My n̶a̶m̶e̶ ̶w̶a̶s̶ ̶N̶e̶l̶l̶a̶, but everyone called me Duck. When I was six years old, the teacher in our four-room school read a story from a book. It had a hard green cover and the pages were creased and some of the pages were torn. I already knew how to read, which set me apart from the other students in class. The story was called *The Ugly Duckling*, and it was about a little duck who looked different from the others, but who turned into a beautiful swan at the end. Or something like that.

Maybe my mother meant well when she called me Duck, thinking that my ugliness was temporary, that I would someday be the swan in the family. Then again, there already was a swan in the Dukes clan: Merline. Ours was a house of women, no fathers or brothers, and I used to hope that calling me Duck was their way of making me feel better about being the ugly sister.

The day the teacher read the story, I asked Merline about it.

"People said you had the biggest nose they'd ever seen on a newborn. They called it a duck's bill. And for the ugly part, well, look in the mirror." Merline walked away, laughing.

SWAN

AFRICA FINE

Genesis Press, Inc.

INDIGO LOVE SPECTRUM

An imprint of Genesis Press, Inc.
Publishing Company

Genesis Press, Inc.
P.O. Box 101
Columbus, MS 39703

Copyright © 2010 Africa Fine

ISBN: 13 DIGIT : 978-1-58571-377-6
ISBN: 10 DIGIT : 1-58571-377-5
Manufactured in the United States of America

First Edition

Visit us at www.genesis-press.com
or call at 1-888-Indigo-1-4-0

DEDICATION

"We are each other's magnitude and bond."

GWENDOLYN BROOKS (1917–2000)

ACKNOWLEDGMENTS

Although *Swan* is a work of fiction, I made an effort to place my fictional characters in settings that were faithful to places and times. Several books and authors were particularly helpful, including:

Haskins, James. *Black Music in America: A History Through Its People.* New York: Thomas Y. Crowell, 1987.

Huey, Brenda. *The Blackest Land, The Whitest People: Greenville Texas.* Bloomington: AuthorHouse, 2006.

Spinney, Robert G. *City of Big Shoulders: A History of Chicago.* DeKalb: Northern Illinois University Press, 2000.

Ward, Geoffrey C. and Ken Burns. *Jazz: A History of America's Music.* New York: Alfred A. Knopf, 2000.

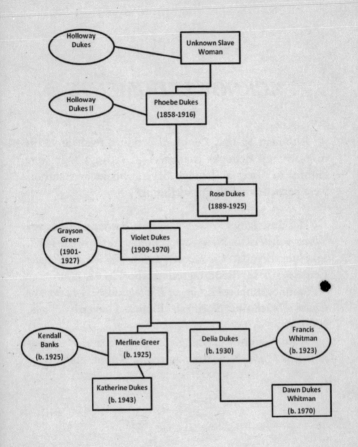

DUKES FAMILY TREE

CHAPTER 1

"Blues in the Night"

Duck
Greenville, 1942

I spent my childhood in Hunt County, Texas, in a town called Greenville. It was a place that had two sides, the side that it showed to the world, and the side it tried to hide. If you stood on Lee Street facing east, you would see the Greenville Hotel and Crawford's Grocery and Market on the north side of the street. Above all the other signs, you would see a large black banner hanging over the street. "GREENVILLE," it proclaimed in white block lettering. Underneath in smaller letters was the word "Welcome." That is how the people who ran Greenville saw themselves and the town: a place that welcomed visitors and natives to our downtown. We were Southerners, proud Texans who loved our home.

On either side of the words "GREENVILLE" and "Welcome" were two parts of a single phrase. "The Blackest Land" appeared on the left side of the sign. On the right side was the phrase "The Whitest People." Our soil was black and fertile, the best kind of dirt for growing and prospering in an agricultural community.

And our people, well, they saw themselves as clean and honest. White. This was what the people in charge meant to say, but the truth was that this was wishful thinking. I always believed that the white people wished Greenville was a white town, both in morality and population. And maybe if they put up a sign that said so, Negroes would take the hint and move on out. Or maybe visitors would take the sign to mean that while black people might live in Greenville, they weren't the kind that would make waves, complain, demand political power or the right to eat in the same establishments frequented by upstanding, moral white folks. The people who mattered were white. The people who didn't were black.

When I was twelve years old, I didn't know the word *irony*. But I knew that by letting that sign hang on Lee Street for more than forty years, whites in Greenville intended to show their good side; but without meaning to, they showed what was wrong with the town.

Greenville was a town so small that everyone, whites and blacks, was related somehow to everyone else. That did not mean that there was any mixing of the races, at least not in the daytime.

We were sixty miles outside Dallas, which isn't that far, but living in Greenville was like living in another world. While people in the big cities were worried about the Germans, jazz music and the "Negro problem," life in Greenville was the same as always. The town was divided by railroad tracks that hadn't been used in years. The wealthiest people had many acres of land and two- or three-story homes that were called *estates*. Poor whites lived on one side in houses that looked like ours except they all had tiny patches of grass that served as yards. We lived on the other side of the tracks. No one thought to cross over.

We had separate grammar schools, each of which went up to the eighth grade. There were two high schools, one for coloreds and one for whites, but not many black kids graduated. Most had to drop out to work.

Since there weren't many businesses in Greenville, whites and blacks had to share some things. But the white town council divided the hours for all merchants into hours for whites and hours for blacks. That way, the good upstanding citizens of Greenville didn't have to come into contact with us Negroes any more than was necessary. They said it was for our benefit, too, although no one ever explained how or why.

We worked for the whites, of course, doing jobs they didn't want to do, like cleaning and lifting, and working the more dangerous machines in the cotton mill. There was no social contact. We spoke only when spoken to, and there was no room for friendship between blacks and whites.

Greenville was a town full of secrets big and small. Some secrets were truly that, and some were secrets in name only, since everyone knew about them but no one ever talked about them.

I have always known secrets. I knew that Mother loved my sister Merline more than she loved me. I knew that Mother had never loved my father, and I knew that my father and Merline's were not the same man. I knew that although Greenville was segregated in the daytime, there was at least one place on the Negro side of town where rich white women came to drink whiskey and flirt with black men while their husbands were away on business trips. I knew that I could sing better than anyone in the church choir, but I was too shy to let anyone hear me.

During the summer of 1942, when I was twelve and Merline was seventeen, my sister was keeping the biggest secret of all. She didn't tell me, of course. I just knew by the way she acted that something was different. I made it my business to find out.

My name is Delia, but everyone called me Duck. When I was six years old, the teacher in our four-room school read a story from a book. It had a hard green cover and the pages were creased and some of the pages were torn. I already knew how to read, which set me apart from the other students in class. The story was called *The Ugly Duckling*, and it was about a little duck who looked different from the others, but who turned into a beautiful swan at the end. Or something like that.

Maybe my mother meant well when she called me Duck, thinking that my ugliness was temporary, that I would someday be the swan in the family. Then again, there already was a swan in the Dukes clan: Merline. Ours was a house of women, no fathers or brothers, and

I used to hope that calling me Duck was their way of making me feel better about being the ugly sister.

The day the teacher read the story, I asked Merline about it.

"People said you had the biggest nose they'd ever seen on a newborn. They called it a duck's bill. And for the ugly part, well, look in the mirror." Merline walked away, laughing.

Merline was mean. Not just to me—Merline was mean to everyone as far as I could tell. But she was also breathtakingly lovely. By the time she was eleven years old, men regularly stopped to watch her walk by. She grew her hair long and straightened it, using hot irons to curl it into whatever styles were depicted in the movie magazines she stole from Woolworth's. She wore skirts that showed off her calves, and when she got a little older, she wore high heels she bought with money she begged off Mother. She made everyone outside the house call her Merl because she thought it sounded more sophisticated. At fifteen, she started wearing red lipstick despite Mother's disapproving claim that only whores wore red. When I learned the word *irony*, I realized that my sister was a perfect example: ripe on the outside, rotten on the inside.

"Go away, Duck," Mother said when I asked her what a whore was. "You need to be cleaning those dishes instead of asking me foolish questions."

Merline offered her own graphic explanation later, which I did not believe. The things she told me were sick, and I may have been just a kid, but I knew no one would do the things my sister described. Even then, I didn't trust Merline.

Mother put her in charge of my care, like a lieutenant reporting to my mother, the captain. Mother worked long hours at two jobs, cleaning houses on the white side of town, so my sister and I were left alone after school. When I complained that Merline was bossy and unfair, I had two choices: obey my older sister or suffer a beating with a belt, an extension cord or the flat of Mother's hand, depending on her mood.

My mother wasn't the nurturing parent I read about in books. She didn't bake cookies, she didn't let us snuggle up to her on the sofa, and she didn't compliment us. If she was pleased with Merline's looks, she might say, "Girl, that long hair and those eyelashes are going to get you in trouble if you aren't careful."

Or, if Merline made a funny comment, Mother would chuckle and say, "You got a smart mouth on you. That's not from my side of the family."

I can't remember ever doing anything Mother thought worthy of praise, backhanded or otherwise. She only said I reminded her of my father, a man whose name I never knew.

"That man was evil," she used to say. "God blessed me the day he disappeared."

It was a small kindness that she didn't add that leaving me behind was a curse.

Merline's father was different. He was the love of my mother's life, and he had died when Merline was just a baby. I always imagined this was what turned Mother hard, what robbed her of the ability to enjoy even the smallest pleasures. All she would ever say was that she'd loved him, and white people had killed him.

More than the pain, the anger was what made Mother's beatings so hard to take. Still, I was certain that I'd rather take a beating than have my sister order me around, but I knew that if I chose the punishment, Mother would just beat me and Merline would still be in charge.

Usually, my sister ruled me like a drill sergeant under the threat that if I didn't obey, she would tell Mother. During the summers, I had very specific duties that needed to be carried out at various times during the day. These tasks were all my sister's chores in addition to mine. Mother didn't care, as long as everything got done and our house looked like "we'd been brought up right." I hated summers, because I was forced to spend entire days being ordered around like a servant. At least during the school year, I got a break until three in the afternoon.

But that summer of 1942 was different. Merline disappeared for hours at a time every afternoon, leaving me free to do anything I wanted. She never told me she was leaving. I would notice an unusual break in between orders, and I would escape to our room to hide and read once I realized she wasn't there.

I loved reading. I remember the first time I read a book from front to back. It was a Nancy Drew mystery. The existence of that other world amazed me. Nancy Drew wasn't like the white people in Greenville. She didn't use the word *nigger* every other sentence. She drove a convertible and had friends, Beth and George, and even a boyfriend named Ned. She was smart and solved mysteries like no one else could. Her hair was titian blonde, and even though I didn't know what that meant, I knew it was good. I wanted to be Nancy Drew. I didn't think of it as wanting to be white, or not wanting to be black. I just wanted what Nancy had. Freedom. Happiness. Hope.

I was a skinny, dark-skinned black girl called Duck. I didn't know anyone who had gone to college except the teachers at my school. I'd never seen a Negro in a convertible. No one commented on the beauty of my nappy hair, and it certainly wasn't titian blonde. I didn't have any friends; at school, the girls made fun of me when I raised my hand to give the answers and the boys ignored me.

I knew I couldn't be Nancy Drew, so the next best thing was reading about her. Greenville had a tiny library and the white woman who worked behind the desk was nice to me, meaning she didn't call me nigger and didn't laugh when I told her I wanted to borrow books. She kept me stocked with Nancy Drew books as they came out, and I devoured every one of them as if it were my last meal. At first, I didn't care why Merline disappeared those afternoons. I looked at it as a gift from God. More time for me and Nancy.

Under normal circumstances, Merline liked to be the center of attention. She would have hated to think that she was gone and no one even noticed. But that summer was different. Merline had a secret. It wasn't until she started sneaking out at night that I got interested in what she was doing.

It was a mystery that I decided to solve, just as Nancy Drew would have.

For several days, I did everything Merline told me to without any argument at all. And I watched her. She left the house around two o'clock every afternoon. From our bedroom window, I watched her look around before walking down the dirt road toward the railroad tracks. While I read about Nancy, I kept an eye on the clock and an ear out for Mother. Merline returned just before five o'clock, when it was time to start cooking dinner, or more precisely, time to order me to start dinner. Mother never got home before nine o'clock from work, so she didn't have the time to keep tabs on my sister. But I did.

At night, Merline's pattern changed. She waited to leave until my breathing became regular and she thought I was asleep. I learned to keep still, my eyes slits as I watched her put on her best dress, dab perfume on her throat and, carrying her heels in her hand, climb out of our window. I didn't want her to see me in the moonlight, so I stood to the side of the window and peeked out to see her hurrying down the dirt road in the same direction she'd taken in the afternoon.

The mystery had three parts: Who was she going to see, where was she going, and why was that place in the opposite direction from where everyone we knew lived? Our house, a narrow structure called a shotgun, was separated from most others. We were close to the edge of the Negro neighborhoods, not far from the tracks. But there was nowhere to go once you reached the tracks. On the other side were the white people. No black person would cross those tracks.

At least, not in the daytime.

But what about at night? The one Negro bar in Greenville, the Top Hat, held dances that Mother had forbidden Merline to attend. At first, I thought she was sneaking out to meet one of the boys who drank there while listening to the jazz music that I loved and Mother said was sinful. Once I had seen her go in the opposite direction three nights in a row, I knew Merline wasn't going to the Top Hat.

Once I was sure of Merline's patterns, which never changed over a week, I thought about my next move. What would Nancy do? What Nancy would do, I decided, was follow Merline. It wouldn't work in the afternoon, when the sun provided too much light for stealth. But at night, she was so involved in reaching her secret destination that she might not catch me following. Because footsteps on the dirt road sounded like rasping breaths, I knew I would have to stay far enough back so that my own footsteps would get lost in the sound of Merline's. I would need to wear something dark and hug the trees that lined either side of the road. I would need to catch just a glimpse of my sister's destination, and then head back home so I would be sleeping by the time she returned. Most of all, she could never know I had done this. I knew she would never tell Mother. That would mean revealing her own secret as well, and it was clear that she didn't want anyone—especially Mother—to know. But Merline had ways of getting revenge. I did not want to experience the full brunt of her rage.

I decided to follow her on a Friday night. I figured this was the best chance of catching something interesting going on. Mother always said that the worst sinning happened on Saturday nights, and that was why the Second Baptist Church on our side of town (the whites claimed First Baptist as their own) was full every Sunday morning. Not that my mother had firsthand knowledge of this. She wouldn't set foot in a church, claiming that it was full of hypocrites, and, if there was a God, he would be aghast at what people did in his name.

But Merline stayed in on Saturday nights. Either she wasn't sinning, or Mother was wrong.

It was a still July night during one of the hottest summers anyone could remember. The temperature passed 100 degrees during the afternoons, and the nights cooled to the upper eighties. After those hot days, the nights, as still and dry as they were, felt like a cool breeze.

The room I shared with Merline was the hottest in the house because it was the smallest, and, somehow, no breeze ever passed through the window even when left wide open. Our house was long and narrow, the kind of wooden structure that people used to say you could shoot from the front door and have the buckshot end up in the backyard. It was built of sturdy wooden planks that had been painted white when the house was new. All the rooms were small and connected to the next. The front door opened into a tiny living room. Next was the kitchen, then the room I shared with Merline. A bathroom separated our room from Mother's, which had a door going to the tiny patch of dirt out back. It might have had a certain charm when it was new, but it had not been renovated since it was built to house workers at nearby ranches and estates in the 1800s. The walls needed painting inside and out, the rooms were cramped instead of cozy, and the hardwood floors were scratched and worn throughout the house.

Though the space was limited, Merline and I made the best of what we had. Each of us claimed a side of the room. On my side, I kept used books I had bought for pennies at library sales, a radio and all my school assignments from the past year. I liked for things to be neat, so I stacked everything on shelves made from wooden milk crates. There was no money for fancy bedspreads, so I used an old faded pink chenille bedspread we had in the closet. My bed was always neatly made when I wasn't in it, and I even lined up my two pairs of shoes neatly in front of the armoire we shared.

In the dusty area underneath my bed, I kept my prized possession, a cheap plastic radio that I listened to whenever I could, keeping the volume low and whispering the words to the songs I loved. I had begged for the radio for the better part of two years before Mother finally allowed me to have one, and after Merline made fun of me for singing along to the music, I kept the radio, and my singing, hidden from her derisive eyes.

Merline's side of the room looked like a tornado had just whirled through, spreading her belongings up to the line we marked in tape down the middle of the floor. She had no shelves or books, and what papers she kept from school were either stuffed in her satchel or shoved under the bed. Merline's prized possessions were her fashion and movie magazines. She liked to pore over them and then arrange her own hair or dress in the styles of the women featured in the photos. She hid her lipstick in the armoire inside a shoebox, which I knew because, before I decided to follow Merline, I looked through her things one afternoon for clues to her secret.

My own hiding place was much more clever. I had acquired two used copies of *Huckleberry Finn*, and even though I hated to ruin a book, I hollowed out a small space in the one that the most worn and stuck it back on my makeshift bookshelf. I knew no one in my family would ever find anything I hid there, because I had never seen Merline or Mother so much as glance at a book unless under duress. I had no treasures to put in there yet, but when the time came, I would be prepared. The night I set out to follow Merline, I was confident I would find out what was going on. Someone who had such an obvious hiding place couldn't keep a secret from me.

The town had celebrated Independence Day last week and now that the smell of fireworks had faded from the air, everyone was getting back to normal. The house was still as it ever got, which means I could hear Mother mumbling in her sleep at the other end of the house. I didn't even bother to watch Merline get ready. I didn't want to tip her off in any way, didn't want to risk what I had come to think of as my operation. During lulls between Nancy Drew books, I had taken to reading detective novels. The librarian called them pulps and said I was probably too young for them. I told her I was taking them home to Mother, a lie I knew would work because, as far as I could tell, Mother never even read the newspaper, let alone a book from the library.

In these little novels, the detectives always mounted operations to catch someone in a lie or a crime. I decided that what I had here had started out as a simple Nancy Drew caper, but with my surveillance (a word I learned from the pulps) plans, the status was raised to the level of an official operation.

There was a moment when Merline, about to climb out the window, looked back at me, her shoes hanging in her hand as usual. I froze. I felt my heart thump in my chest. I was sure my breathing changed, that the sound of the blood rushing through my head was audible to Merline.

"Duck. You awake?"

She must have been truly worried if she was willing to risk a night out to make sure I wasn't watching. It was more important for her not to get caught than to go out on this particular night.

I tried to keep my breathing steady. Then, I thrashed, mumbled and turned over in my bed, my back to Merline. I wanted her to see the rise and fall of my torso. I wanted her to be sure I was asleep.

"Duck?"

Rise and fall. Rise and fall.

Merline's feet made a soft thump as she climbed over the windowsill and dropped softly to the ground.

I waited as long as I could before I threw off the covers and followed her.

Kendall Banks was one of the palest white people I'd ever seen. Most white people grew tanned in the Texas sun—from working outside at their jobs, from mowing the lawn, from walking down the block to the store. Old people became leathery and browner than some of the Negroes. Babies had rosy brown faces and limbs. Teenage boys were almost always the tannest. They played baseball in the spring and football in the fall, and the practices darkened their skin almost as soon as the seasons began.

But Kendall Banks was the only white person I'd ever seen who was pale, his hair almost white, his eyes the color of freshly cut grass. His skin didn't tan and it didn't burn. At first, I thought it must be because he always wore a Texas Tech baseball cap perched atop his head. But then I looked at his arms—they should have been the color of oak and they weren't. His family members were all blonde, too, but they tanned just like the other white people.

Kendall went by Kenny, and he was one of the privileged few in our town who had never worked a day in their lives. His hands were soft and white, and his clothes were always immaculate, even on the hottest days. In some places, the most respected people were professionals: teachers, doctors, lawyers. In Greenville, cotton was king. The Banks family made their money first in cotton, then in railroads to transport the cotton all over the country. When those opportunities dried up, the family invested in Majors Airport and defense contracting during the wars. If there was a way to make money, Kenny's father found it, and by the time Merline and Kenny were seventeen, Kendall Banks Sr.'s empire was so well-established that Kenny would never have to work a day in his life. If Greenville had royalty, Kendall Senior, his wife, Nancy, and their only child, Kenny, were it.

Even though I had no relationships with white people outside of the librarian, I knew who Kenny Banks was. I overheard my mother and a woman she worked with gossiping about the people whose houses they cleaned. Miss Myra cleaned houses for the Bankses, a good job, she said, because they were clean and decent.

"For white folks, anyway," she would say, a high-pitched cackle bursting from her lips.

"Little Kenny is a catch. He comes and goes all hours of the day and night, helping his father, he says. I think he's got a girlfriend."

Mother didn't say much, but Myra started talking about which white family had more money, whose wife was cheating and whose husband beat her, and no more was said about the Banks family. That was the last time I thought about Kenny before the night I followed Merline.

If you walked quickly in a straight line from our house toward the tracks, it wouldn't take more than fifteen minutes. But Merline didn't take a straight path. Instead, she wove in and out of the woods on either side of the road, meandering, and sometimes stopping, with her head tilted, as if listening for a signal.

All I heard was the sound of crickets and, occasionally, a mockingbird's medley. We had learned in school that the mockingbird mimicked the calls of several other birds in its song. My teacher said the mockingbird had the prettiest song of any bird she'd ever heard. We had been walking for more than twenty minutes before it occurred to me that I shouldn't hear the call of a mockingbird after midnight. I was pretty sure that birds had to sleep, too, especially since they awoke so early.

Just then, Merline stood still. The false birdcall sounded again, and she quickened her pace. Soon she crossed the tracks, then veered into the woods on the white side. I followed, but I lost her in the brush. I could hear her steps, then whispers, but I wasn't sure from what direction the sounds had come. I could almost make out the words, so I knew my sister and her secret were close by.

I kept still, afraid that if I moved they would hear me as clearly as I could hear them. I had suspected that Merline's strange behavior involved a man, but not someone like Kenny Banks. Not a *white* man.

There was a long silence, then I heard a soft moan. I took a chance and crept closer. I told myself that Merline might be hurt, that it was my duty to help my sister. I knew the truth was that Merline deserved a little pain for the way she treated me.

The moans grew louder. The sound was directly to my right on the other side of a group of wide birch bushes. I slipped closer, easing open a slot in the cinnamon-colored branches.

They were in a little clearing, lying on plump blankets that must have come from his home because we didn't own anything as sumptuous. There was a picnic basket nearby. Merline's hands were empty when she left home, and I wondered what kind of a man brought food for a woman instead of the other way around. My mind was racing and I could feel my breath quicken. There was so much to take in, so much that was unfamiliar and frightening.

They both lay on their sides, facing each other, kissing. They were fully clothed, but his hands roamed all over my sister's body. Those were her moans I heard, and she wasn't hurt. I squinted to see for sure, and yes, it was true: my sister was *smiling*. She most often bore a frowning smirk on her face, as if the world were a constant disappointment that she had learned to expect. As I watched, her brow was smooth and relaxed. Mean Merline was pretty. Happy Merline was breathtaking.

This was such a revelation that it took a few more moments for it to fully register that Merline was sneaking off to meet a white man. His back was to me, but I recognized him. Merline was lying there kissing Kenny Banks.

I knew I should look away, go back home, plan my next move, if there was any move to be made. Instead, I stayed. I watched Kenny peel off my sister's clothes with a gentleness I didn't know men could possess. I watched them melt together in the moonlight. I watched them giggle together afterward as they ate from the picnic basket.

It was a lovely scene, the first time I knew what the word *romance* really meant.

It was a terrifying scene. It was the first time I felt true fear.

I was afraid that Merline would get hurt. I was afraid of what Mother would say. I was afraid no one would ever look at me the way Kenny Banks looked at my sister.

When Merline began to dress, I left, keeping quiet until I reached the road. It was then that I took off running. I needed to beat her home, true, but I was running from the idea of the whole thing as well. If I could run fast enough, the sense of foreboding would stay behind, unable to match the pace I set.

When I arrived home, I sneaked back into our room and got under the covers, my body still damp with sweat from running, my heart still pounding. I lay there listening for Merline's soft steps, thinking about secrets. Children know better than anyone the nature of secrets kept and revealed. When one child tells another a secret, it requires a sacred trust, sometimes sealed with complicated vows, and if only two children knew, the secret is safe. But when more than two people knew the secret, it will get out sooner or later.

I was the third person to know Merline's secret, which meant that others would find out, too. I didn't plan on telling, but I knew I didn't have to. There was something about too many people knowing a secret that made it impossible to keep. The knowledge thrived like poison ivy without anyone realizing, or even intending, its spread.

This secret wasn't like the others I knew. This one would hurt someone. Merline. Mother. Me.

I thought I would never fall asleep that night, maybe never sleep again. But my eyes closed and I drifted off well before Merline climbed through the window and back into her bed.

CHAPTER 2

"Who Wouldn't Love You?"

Merline
Greenville, 1942

Kenny's hands glided over Merline's skin. If hands could whisper, this is what it would feel like. The skin on her arms tingled as his fingers passed. The skin on her neck tickled as his hands lingered. Her lips pouted when his swept over hers, too brief, too soft. She wanted more, but he would make her wait. She demanded more, but he just smiled and kept his pace slow, never daring too much.

That night in July was their first time. Merline's first time. No one ever told her to, but she had the idea that she would wait for the man she loved. She didn't think of it as her first love. Merline believed love only happened once. Real love only happened once. Kenny was real love.

He smelled like fresh-squeezed lemonade with a hint of mint in it. He smelled like pine trees and fresh-cut grass. He smelled like popcorn and bubble bath and spring. Kenny Banks smelled like everything good. Before she met him, Merline never knew that goodness had its own fragrance.

They had known each other since they were seven years old. Each day, Merline strayed away from her house and went into the woods, where she was working on creating what another girl might have called a fort or a secret hideaway. Merline called hers a salon. She told Mother all about it, but made it seem like an imaginary place.

"Girl, you spend a lot of time putting on airs."

Mother smirked and took a drag on her cigarette. Duck, a chunky toddler, was propped up on the floor with pillows, sucking from a bottle and humming a tune Merline couldn't identify.

"A salon! Please."

Merline smiled as if she also thought the idea was ridiculous. It was not. The salon was not just in her imagination. It was a real place that she had set up in the woods, using old sheets to make a tent and a straw broom to clear the ground. Merline's salon was a place where a woman of her stature could groom herself in the dressing room (created using a partition made of a flattened box and decorated with painted flowers). In the salon's main room, Merline would entertain guests. They would sit on the swept floor, legs crossed, while drinking tea from mugs she stole from the back of Mother's cabinet. Merline wasn't sure how to make tea, but she knew it was essential to offer it to guests in her salon.

Kenny was her first guest.

He was building his own sanctuary in the woods and that's how he happened upon Merline's salon. Kenny thought it was a good idea to cross over to the colored side of the tracks to build his; none of his friends would think to look for him there. He called his a study. A study was where real men went for privacy, something he yearned for. Though he lived in a big house, his mother was always hovering around him, worrying about him, watching him. She had no other children to keep her busy, and by age seven, her singular attention to Kenny's every movement was oppressive. So, he created a study. Men smoked pipes and read the newspaper in the study, which is why he was holding a stack of old newspapers he'd collected when he came face-to-face with Merline in the woods.

She was holding a piece of calico she planned to use as a tablecloth. They stood looking at each other, neither sure what to say. Mother always told Merline to avert her eyes when she passed a white man. That's how black girls stayed safe. But Kenny wasn't a man, he was a boy, the same size as Merline. He had freckles on his pale skin, and his eyebrows were so white they blended in with his skin. He had the kind of upturned nose Merline had seen on boys named Bobby and Jack in her elementary school textbooks. He smelled of lemons.

"Hi."

Kenny smiled and held out his hand, but it was awkward because he still held the old newspapers. Merline paused for a moment, startled. She had never shaken hands with anyone, let alone a white person. Was he making fun of her? She wasn't sure, but she held out her own hand anyway, and some of his newspapers fell on the ground while their palms clasped.

Merline bent over to help him pick up the papers and his fingers brushed her hand. She looked up at him and smiled.

"Want to come see my salon? It's right over there." She pointed toward the center of the woods.

"You have a salon out here? I have a study."

They became friends.

As a teenager, Merline was one of only a few Negro girls her age who didn't work cleaning houses, washing clothes, or whatever white people needed done. Mother said she would be of more use watching over Duck, who was a nuisance except that she gave Merline a way out of manual labor. Mother doted on Merline and ignored Duck, but Merline believed the special attention was just. When she looked in the mirror, she liked what she saw and thought that if anyone deserved to be the favorite, it was Merline.

Kenny told her she was beautiful. They were in the place where her old salon had been the first time he said it. The salon was no longer there; they were fourteen and Merline was too old to play pretend games. But she was old enough to dream of a real salon, in a real house of her own. The salon was gone, but this was still their secret place, where they came to talk about things they couldn't tell anyone else.

Kenny told her about his father, a man who was loved by everyone except his family. To them, he was a tyrant—exacting, demanding, terrifying. When things weren't perfect, and they hardly ever were, his father went into rages that left Kenny's mother with bruises down her

back and legs. He never hit her in the face. He abused
Kenny in a different way. Kendall Banks Sr. told Kenny
he would follow in his footsteps, take over Banks, Inc.,
marry a Texas belle, settle down right here in Greenville.
According to his father, Kenny would be just like his
father. The thought of it made Kenny sick to his
stomach.

Merline told him about her little sister Duck, who
was smarter than anyone Merline had ever known. She
told him how scary this was, because Duck's intelligence
made it hard for her to get along with people. She told
him that Mother didn't favor Duck because her father
was a man that Mother wished she'd never met. Duck
looked just like him, and while her little sister was
starting to grow out of her awkward looks, Mother still
saw that man whenever she looked at Duck.

The first time Kenny told Merline she was beautiful,
it was August. The woods provided secrecy and shady
cover from the heat. Kenny was going to high school in
a month and so was Merline, but their schools were, of
course, far from each other at opposite ends of the town.
She cried because going into high school seemed like the
end of something rather than a beginning. She cried
because she hated school. She cried because she knew
that there would be less time to spend with Kenny in the
woods, and she would be stuck in the house with Duck,
a twelve-year-old nuisance whose intelligence made
Merline feel dumb.

She cried because she would lose Kenny. She knew
their friendship wasn't right. If it was right, they wouldn't

have to keep it secret. She also knew that Kenny was becoming a man. Being friends with a white boy was one thing. With a white man, it was impossible.

"But Merl, you don't need to worry about Duck, about school, about me. You're beautiful." He nodded as he said it. His tone was solemn.

She wasn't sure what this meant. She didn't care. It was the first time he'd ever called her Merl. It was the first time he ever called her beautiful. Merl leaned over and kissed Kenny on the lips. Then she ran away, out of the woods, straight home.

All Merline's life, a sign hung over Lee Street in downtown Greenville. It read: "The Blackest Land, the Whitest People." When Merline was a small girl, she had asked her mother what it meant.

"That's just white people trying to convince themselves of something that's not true," Mother had said with a bitter laugh.

It was a long time before Merline knew what her mother had meant, and anyway, she never thought much about race issues. Of course, she heard whispers about people getting in trouble over race in Georgia and Alabama. Merline was happy to be who she was because beauty made everything easier. Men, both Negro and white, watched her walk down the street, and she knew that if she wanted any one of them, nothing would get in her way—not the rules about whites being separate from blacks and not a sign that pretended she didn't exist in her own hometown.

Merline had embraced this womanly power from the moment she was old enough to let her hips sway when she walked. At age seventeen, she didn't have any specific plans about life (Duck was the planner in the family, not Merline), but she never doubted that her beauty would take her far in life.

She knew she was pregnant right away, before there were any signs. There was a moment when two things became clear as she lay in bed listening to Duck's even breathing and thinking about Kenny. She was in love with Kenny, and she was pregnant.

The panic rose softly, creeping up through her body until she feared the entire house could hear her heart beating. True, Merline didn't have a plan for what she would do after high school, but it was August before her senior year, and she had figured there was plenty of time left.

Now, she was faced with the impossible. She was in love with a white man, a white man who knew her body almost better than she did. She loved everything about him, from the smell of his skin to his bowlegged stance. She loved his white blond hair and the way he called her Merl. She couldn't imagine not loving him, and she couldn't imagine having his child.

Merline heard the first birds chirping in the trees when she finally closed her eyes and prayed for sleep. She dreamed of the sign all night: The Blackest Land. The Whitest People.

Merline kept her secret for four weeks, hoping she was wrong about the baby, but knowing she wasn't. The weekend before Labor Day, she met Kenny at their usual place. He brought a blanket and a bottle of champagne that he'd stolen from his father's cabinet.

Merline watched him pour, but wouldn't meet his eyes.

"What are we celebrating?" She tried to make her voice sound casual, like the old Merline. But that girl was gone, replaced by someone whose breasts were tender, someone who had dark circles under her eyes from lying awake all night, trying not to think.

"I always feel like celebrating when I'm with you," Kenny said. He was teasing her. Four weeks ago, this would have made her laugh.

She stared into her glass, watching the bubbles burst against each other. Kenny put his finger under her chin and gently lifted it so that her eyes met his.

"What's wrong, Merl?"

She took a deep breath and tried to think of a lie, anything that would keep her from having to say the truth aloud. Kenny's face was kind and worried, and when he gave her a sad smile, she burst into tears, leaning into his arms.

"What is it? Tell me, Merl. You're worrying me."

"I'm pregnant."

Merline's face was pressed against his chest, and she could feel his heart begin to race. Now he would say the things she had dreamed about, the ugly words that narrated her nightmares and made her afraid to fall asleep.

He would talk about how it was impossible, how they had been wrong to be together in the first place, how he couldn't be a father to a mulatto child.

"We'll get married."

Merline pulled away and looked at him. She had never seen him smile like this. His whole face was flushed with excitement.

"I love you, Merl. And I'll love our baby. We can figure out a way to make it work, I know it."

It was the first time he said he loved her, and for a moment, she let herself feel the thrilled trembling in her stomach. They were in love, and surely there was something special about that, right? Surely, that mattered more than the color of their skin? Surely, this baby was a blessing, just as all babies were. Isn't that what people said about babies, that they were blessings from God? A baby made from love, what could be more important?

But Merline, foolishly in love and pregnant, was a practical girl. She might not read all the time the way Duck did, but she knew how Greenville worked. The blackest land. The whitest people.

"Kenny, we can't get married."

"Why not?"

Suddenly, Merline realized that Kenny didn't believe there were limits to what he could do. He was the only child of wealthy parents, the golden child who was doted upon by his family and the entire town. He lived his entire life being told he could, and would, be and do what he wanted. Being the son of Kendall Banks Sr. guaranteed his freedom, and he honestly believed that his privilege would allow him to ignore the rules of life, of Greenville. That kind of belief in the limitless possibilities of life was foreign to Merline. She knew that no matter how much she dreamed, there were limits to what she could do, who she could become. Every Negro Merline knew understood this basic truth about the world in 1942. Kenny was living in a different world from Merline's if he thought they could get married.

"Get married where? It's not even legal in Texas for Negroes and whites to marry."

Kenny shrugged. "So we'll go somewhere where it is legal." He took her hands in his and leaned forward, his voice low and urgent.

"I'll take care of you, Merl. And I'll take of our baby. We'll figure out a way to be together. You'll see. You just have to trust me."

Merline looked at him for a long while. He seemed young to her, much younger than she, even though he would turn eighteen in a few weeks. She could see he really believed what he was saying.

She wanted to believe him, to accept his word and give in to the hope she had spent weeks trying to keep from growing into pure delusion. And here was Kenny, his clear emerald eyes shining, his brow so certain, putting his hand over her still-flat tummy.

"I love you." It was all she could imagine saying.

Merline let Kenny's kisses transport her to the place where they were the only two people in the world.

Merline wished she had known that day, when she was just four months pregnant, that she wouldn't see Kenny again for ten years. She might have said more, might have tried harder to make him understand that having the baby and getting married wasn't a real option. She might have explained to him that the sign over Lee Street was more than just a sign. Or maybe, if she had known what was coming, she wouldn't have told Kenny she was pregnant at all. She would have focused on the feeling of his breath on her cheek, the smell of his hair.

Every night during the next week, she went to their secret place. At times, she got the feeling someone was watching, but all she ever saw were long shadows cast by the trees. Kenny was never there. One night she waited for hours, waited so long the sky was turning from indigo to charcoal by the time she sneaked back in through the bedroom window. The previous night, she thought she saw Duck's eyes move underneath her lids.

"Duck?"

Merline felt the unfamiliar desire to talk to her little sister, to tell her everything, to ask why Kenny hadn't come to their place. It was hard to keep a secret alone, and without Kenny, the secret of the baby weighed her down. He said he loved her. He said they would figure out a way, and a tiny part of her heart had believed him. That was part of her love for him, that she believed he could make everything okay. And now, she needed someone, even Duck, to reassure her that it might be possible, that love might be like it is in the movies, that love might be more important than money, more important than skin color.

"Duck?" But her sister's breathing remained deep and regular.

Merline began her senior year in high school the next day, September 8, 1942. Merline usually looked forward to the first day of school if only because it meant she would get out of the house, away from Duck and Mother. Because she lived without a father and the Dukes women had no money to speak of, she wasn't at the top of the heap at the all-black high school. She got by on her looks; every boy wanted to kiss her and every girl wanted to be her. It meant she had few close girl-friends but many casual friends, and school was a place where she could gossip about hair and movies, unlike at home, where Mother was always working and Duck kept her head stuck in a book. Merline was just a fair student, mostly because she didn't see how algebra and poetry had anything to do with real life.

This year, people noticed that Merline seemed qui-eter. During homeroom, she rushed to the bathroom without asking to be excused and when she came back, she looked queasy and wan. Each day, she managed to smile and pretend that she was just the same Merline as she'd always been.

That first day of her senior year in high school, Merline learned that Louisiana Senator Huey P. Long had been shot seven years ago. She learned that she would have to read *Huckleberry Finn* in English class. She learned that she hated her math teacher.

And she learned that Kenny Banks was gone, sent off to boarding school by his parents.

By December, anyone could see that Merline was pregnant. She remained as haughty and emotionally aloof as ever, so no one asked her directly about the baby. But they all talked among themselves, and the word spread to her classmates' parents, aunts, uncles and cousins. It wasn't long before Mother, who worked long hours and often didn't lay eyes on her children during waking hours, heard about it.

Merline wasn't sleeping well by that time. She had heard that being pregnant made a woman tired, and that she was, but sleep was hard to come by. Instead, she lay awake nights thinking of Kenny, wondering what he was doing in the fancy boarding school back East. Did he think of her? Why didn't he write? Was he relieved to be away from the burden of a black girl and a mulatto baby? Or was he staying awake night as she was, thinking of her but powerless to change what had already been done?

Duck was the only person who Merline had told about the baby. One sleepless night, Duck had startled her by speaking out into the dark silence of their shared room.

"Do you miss him?"

Merline turned her head on the pillow, wondering how her little sister knew she wasn't asleep. She could see Duck in the light of the moon, lying on her back, staring at the ceiling. She noticed how proud and straight Duck's nose was in profile, and for the first time, she thought that Duck might not be as ugly as they all thought.

"During the day, I keep busy so I don't think of him," Merline replied. She didn't have to add the second half, that the nights were the worst. Duck nodded in the shadows.

"How did you know about us?" Merline had thought she and Kenny were so careful, that no one knew about them.

Duck didn't answer for a long while.

"I know lots of things. People forget about me," she finally explained.

Merline thought about this. Duck had always been smart, everyone knew that. But everyone also knew that being smart didn't get a woman far in life. It was being pretty that mattered. Or that's what Merline had always thought, what the world had always confirmed, what Mother, inadvertently, taught when she tried to keep Merline from emphasizing her beauty.

But then again, it wasn't Duck who was lying awake every night, wondering how she was going to raise a child on her own, wondering what that child would look like, wondering how on earth she could survive tomorrow, forget about the future.

"What else do you know?" Merline whispered.

She could feel Duck watching her now, but it was Merline's turn to stare at the ceiling.

"I know that you need to figure out what you're going to do about everything. When Mother finds out . . ." Duck's words trailed off.

Merline knew the rest. Mother would give her a beating. Or worse. She had always told Merline that beauty was a blessing and a curse, and that the worst thing a woman could do was "give the milk away for free." Well, she had given Kenny the milk, the bucket, the cow and the whole farm.

Instead of answering, Merline turned her back and pretended to sleep. Duck called her name a few times, then gave up. And now, just a week later, someone had seen the bump on Merline's stomach and run tattling to Mother.

Merline arrived home from school in a foul mood, with a queasy stomach and an aching back. She went to the kitchen to see if there was any honey in the house. She was craving honey, and she hoped to just open the bottle and pour it into her mouth.

Mother was standing at the sink, arms folded, a black scowl on her face. She wasn't supposed to be home. She usually worked until ten o'clock at night. Yet, today, there she was, home by three in the afternoon, ready for a fight.

Merline stopped short in the doorway. Her hands took on a life of their own, tugging at the hem of her loose blouse, pulling it out over her belly.

"Do you have something to tell me?" Mother's voice was low, full of bitter rage.

Merline couldn't find her voice. She shook her head.

"No? Are you sure? Because the rest of this nosy town has told me plenty."

Merline's heart thumped loudly and panic rose in her throat. She shook her head, as if denial were a legitimate option.

"What are you trying to hide?" Mother nodded toward Merline's stomach and stepped toward her. Merline took a step back into the next room, the kitchen. She noticed an extension cord sitting on the table, coiled into a neat bundle. Mother picked it up and strode quickly across the room. Before Merline could react, her mother had unfurled the cord and was whipping the cord into the air. Merline fell to the floor and crouched, trying to protect her middle, trying to protect the baby.

"No. Daughter. Of. Mine. Will. Whore. Around." Mother punctuated every word with a blow. Merline concentrated on what she was saying, listening for Kenny's name. But Mother never said anything about the father, never even asked Merline. When her mother's arm grew tired, she issued a final command.

"You get out of this house, and don't ever think about coming back. Whoever fathered that bastard you're carrying can take care of you now."

Mother left Merline cowering on the floor. She would have been surprised to see the bitter smile that emerged through Merline's tears. Mother didn't know about Kenny. She didn't know the most important secret that Merline had, and that meant that no one else knew, either. She found some small comfort in knowing that however disgraceful she was for getting pregnant, no one knew the even bigger disgrace, that the father was a white man. They didn't know she loved Kenny, even though he was gone, maybe forever. That was the small victory she held on to as she packed a small bag and wandered away from her home.

Merline didn't have a destination in mind when she left. There was really nowhere to go, except maybe church, where they would have to take her in even though she was a sinner. But Merline didn't go to church and she wasn't sure she believed in God, although she never really thought it through enough to declare herself an atheist. When people talked about relying on the Lord to get them through hard times, Merline scoffed and swore she would never sit around waiting for an invisible savior to fix everything. When people testified about the power of prayer, Merline wondered how a sane God could let so many Christians suffer. When people asked if she was saved, she smiled vaguely and nodded, thinking that no one was saved from the worst thing, which was death.

She just wandered along the road aimlessly until she saw Duck coming toward her on the path. As always, Duck carried a book in one hand, and in the other she held a brown paper bag. Merline tried to smile at Duck, but she tasted tears on her lips and realized she was crying. Duck didn't say anything, just pulled Merline to the side of the path and made her sit down under the shade of a tree.

It was mid-December, but the weather was still balmy. The weather reports on the radio claimed it was the warmest winter on record, and some people half joked that the heat was the work of the devil.

They sat for a long while without talking. Duck offered Merline half a sandwich from the paper bag and some water, and Merline realized that she was ravenous. After the sandwich was gone, Merline spoke.

"Mother knows."

"About Kenny and the baby?"

"Just about the baby."

Duck sighed. "That's good. If she knew about Kenny, who knows what she'd do."

Mother hated white people. It wasn't just the usual resentment most blacks had toward the pale masses who controlled everything in one way or another. Mother's eyes burned with personal rage against whites whether or not she knew them personally. She had always warned Merline not even to make eye contact with whites, especially the men.

One of Merline's favorite things had been staring into Kenny's green eyes.

"She kicked me out."

Duck raised her eyebrows but did not look surprised. "Where are you going to go?"

Merline shrugged. "I was just out here walking, trying to figure that out."

Duck picked up a blade of grass and chewed on it, thinking.

"I have an idea," she said slowly. "You might not like it. But I can't think of anything better."

Merline looked at her twelve-year-old sister, a girl she had treated poorly her entire life. Why would she help me, Merline thought. If the situation was reversed, would she offer to help Duck? Merline knew the answer was no. She felt an odd mixture of gratitude and hatred toward her little sister. She wanted to spit at her, to ridicule Duck for daring to suppose *she* could help Merline. She hated

Duck for being a better person than her, and she hated herself for needing her little sister's help.

Then she looked down the path and wondered how long she would have walked if Duck hadn't come along. Merline didn't have the slightest idea. So she listened.

The Bankses lived in an imposing two-story mansion that sat on ten acres of land. The back of the home, beyond the expanse of the neatly trimmed yard, was a lush wooded area. The front featured a winding driveway that led up to the Greek Revival-style home that Kendall Banks had built for his wife. Painted a creamy white, the house featured full-height porches on the first and second floors, stone columns stood on either side of the entryway, and every window was framed with shutters painted chocolate brown.

Looking up at the windows, Merline wondered how many rooms were in the house. With only three people living there, she thought it must be lonely to wander around in such a big house. Then she thought of the cramped room she had shared with Duck all her life. Maybe there was something to be said for having too much space.

The walk up the driveway took a lifetime. Merline tried to tamp down the fear rising in her throat. What she was about to do would take a kind of courage she didn't possess. They could laugh in her face, or worse. As she stood at the front door, she felt awkward. She had never entered a white person's home by the main entrance. When she was little, she had sometimes accompanied her mother on cleaning jobs, but they always went through the back door.

There was something else: None of the people whose houses Mother cleaned had ever been home when they were working. Now, she was not only standing at the front door, but she was not here to do a job. She had no idea what to expect, how to say what had to be said.

But there was no choice. She was pregnant and alone. She pushed the doorbell lightly, almost hoping that it wouldn't sound inside the house, that she would have the chance to change her mind and head back the way she'd come.

Kendall Banks Sr. was a tall man with an angular, almost bony face and curly white hair that he kept cropped low. He wore a dark-blue suit, his loosened tie the only indication that it was after dinnertime and he was relaxing for the night. His skin was lightly tanned and freckled, and his hands were as soft as Kenny's. He stood in the doorway, peering down at Merline over the top of his reading glasses. His eyes were emerald like Kenny's, but there was no sparkle or laughter in them. His gaze was calculating and sterile, revealing nothing.

Merline was surprised that Mr. Banks had answered the doorbell. She had expected Kenny's mother to answer, and she had prepared excuses to talk her way into seeing Mr. Banks. Instead, she barely had time to draw her fingers back from the doorbell before he swung open the door, a newspaper grasped in one hand.

She remembered her earlier conversation with Duck.

"Don't beg or plead. If he thinks you're weak, he'll never go along with this," she had said.

Duck had sneaked back into their house to grab Merline's best clothes, what would have been church clothes for another sort of girl. Now, she smoothed down the straight black skirt, wondering if the bump of her belly looked as obvious as it felt. She licked her dry lips before speaking.

"Mr. Banks. My name is Merline Dukes."

Before she could go on, he offered a thin smile.

"I know who you are."

Merline tried to hide her surprise. She had assumed that Kenny would have kept her name a secret, the way she had kept him a secret from Mother.

"Come in."

It was an order, not an invitation. She followed Mr. Banks into the foyer and he pointed toward a room off to the left. She glanced down the hall and saw the back of a woman's dress as its owner swept into the kitchen. Mrs. Banks was quick, but not quick enough to keep Merline from seeing her reddened face and her puffy eyes. That's when she knew that there were no secrets anymore. Kenny, naïve and optimistic, had told his family everything. They had quickly sent him away to boarding school, leaving Merline standing in Mr. Banks's study, alone and pregnant, armed only with her twelve-year-old sister's plan.

"Sit."

Merline obeyed, watching Mr. Banks as he walked over to a shelf and busied himself with lighting a cigar.

The smoke made her feel ill, but her face was a mask and she sat perfectly straight in her chair.

"The baby," she began, gesturing toward her stomach, "is Kenny's."

He blew a long stream of smoke from his lips and smiled, that slight, sardonic smile that was just a curve of the lips. Merline could feel the churning in her belly, a mixture of nausea and fear. It was a mistake to come here. She shouldn't have listened to Duck. What did a little girl know about these things?

"Are you sure about that?" His glasses were still perched down on his nose, as if he was reading Merline's face.

Her teeth clenched and she felt the words rise in her chest. How dare he suggest that she was some kind of tramp, some cheap little girl who slept around. His smile broadened as he watched her try to contain her anger.

"It's Kenny's."

"Let's just say it is. Why did you come here? Kenny is gone away to school, and even if he wasn't, surely you have enough sense to know that there is no happily-ever-after here. " He paused to puff on his cigar once more before crushing the lit end into an ashtray.

"Kenny told me all about you, about the baby. He actually believed that you and he could be together." He gave a raw bark of laughter. "He actually talked about getting married."

Merline looked down at her lap to hide the tears that sprang into her eyes. Since Kenny's disappearance, she had tried not to think about him. It was easier that way.

But now, she remembered how sweetly he'd held her the last time they talked. Kenny was an innocent, someone who truly believed that love made everything okay. For this, Mr. Banks held his son in contempt. But Merline loved him for it.

"I need a place to live. No one knows about me and Kenny, and it can stay that way. But I need a place to live."

She had thought that Mr. Banks would want to keep her out of sight, maybe send her away to another town where she could start a new life. That's what Duck had said would happen, and it sounded reasonable.

He looked at her, his smile gone.

"Are you blackmailing me?" His voice was a hiss, his words dripping with venom.

She shrugged and looked down at her feet before pulling back her shoulders and looking him in the eye. "I'm trying to do what's best. For all of us."

He stood up then, fists clenched at his side, and Merline cringed as he walked toward her.

"She can stay here."

Merline and Mr. Banks froze, then they both turned toward the voice. It was Kenny's mother. Her eyes were still red, but she had on fresh lipstick and her shoulders were squared. She didn't look directly at Merline. Instead, she and her husband held a long look between them, a look that spoke volumes that Merline could not understand.

"She can stay here," Nancy Banks repeated. "It's what's best for the baby."

Mr. Banks narrowed his eyes, glanced down at Merline, and then stalked out of the room. Merline looked at Mrs. Banks, grateful for a place to live but wary of the price she might have to pay.

"You will work for us," Mrs. Banks said, her voice businesslike. She looked at Merline but did not meet her eyes. Instead, her gaze kept returning to Merline's slightly swollen belly. "You'll have to quit school now, anyway, and you'll need to earn a living somehow."

She turned and left the room and Merline followed.

"Thank you," she said to Mrs. Banks's back.

Mrs. Banks turned and finally looked Merline in the eye.

"I'm not doing it for you," she said coldly.

And so, Duck's plan was, in a way, a success.

CHAPTER 3
"All Alone"

Violet
1915–1925

Violet's first memories were of cotton. Not the kind of cotton most people know, those white, fluffy puffs that come neatly packaged in plastic at the grocery store. Not the crisp smoothness of a new T-shirt, nor the gentle luxury of high-thread-count sheets. The cotton Violet remembered was almost beige, flecked with bits of dried sticks and leaves. Freshly picked cotton was messy and could get tangled and stringy unless she was extra careful when she put it in her sack. The cotton plants themselves were green stalks with buds growing on the top. When they were ripe, the plants became brown and the buds opened to produce bits of fluff that someone a long time ago had discovered could be sold at high prices from the High Plains of Texas to people all over the world.

Before Violet was old enough to pick cotton, she had liked the look of the plants, rows and rows of the buds sprouting from the sticks. The crops were low to the ground and when it was time to harvest, the leaves were brown and wrinkled as if the plants were dead. The only signs of life were the bits of fluff bursting from the top of each seed vessel, often making the plants droop with the weight of the cotton.

When she was six years old, her mother brought Violet out into the fields to help work the Dukes farm. Violet's mother, Rose, had grown up on this farm, and her grandmother, Phoebe, had been the property of the Dukes family until 1865. They were sharecroppers, although they never made much more than the worth of their room and board. Phoebe always said it was just slavery called by another name.

Rose said that it didn't matter what it was called, work was work, and Violet was old enough to help out. There was a time, in 1915, when the three of them worked the field together: Phoebe was fifty-seven, Rose was twenty-six, and Violet was just six years old.

When the three of them were out together, picking cotton seemed like an adventure to Violet. They bent over time and again to fill the sacks they each wore slung over their shoulders, dragging a wicker basket behind them. When all three sacks were full, they emptied them into the basket, repeating the process until the basket was full or it was too dark to see their hands working rhythmically over the stalks. The days were hot but filled with chatter and songs sung by Phoebe, whose voice was low and husky, with a smooth vibrato that, when Phoebe held the note just long enough, gave Violet chills.

Phoebe only sang while she was working, claiming that it helped pass the time. She despaired that Rose was tone deaf, but she saw promise in Violet and taught her a few simple songs. One of her favorites was "Amazing Grace," and she taught Violet the lyrics.

Amazing grace. How sweet the sound, that saved a wretch like me. I once was lost but now am found. Was blind, but now I see.

Violet had an idea that white people sang hymns politely, but Phoebe liked to belt out the lyrics at the top of her lungs, usually in the morning when she could count on the mockingbirds to serve as backup singers.

Phoebe urged Violet to sing loudly, to be proud of her tinny soprano. But Violet's voice always drifted off into silence because she loved the sound of her grandmother's voice.

Through many dangers, toils and snares, I have already come. 'Tis grace hath brought me safe thus far, and grace will lead me home.

The only time Phoebe stopped working the cotton was when she sang. She threw her head back, held her straw hat at her side and closed her eyes, serenading the sun.

The three of them never went to church, even though there were some small colored congregations not too far away. Rose claimed that she wanted nothing to do with a God who let slavery happen right under his nose, and Phoebe said she would go for the choir but she needed to rest on Sunday just as the Lord did when he created the world. Violet was glad to have her grandmother and mother all to herself. They were all she needed, and, that first summer she picked cotton, it seemed as if they'd be together forever.

Yea, when this flesh and heart shall fail, and mortal life shall cease, I shall possess, within the veil, a life of joy and peace.

Rose said Phoebe was just showing off when she sang all the verses; most people just sang the first two. Phoebe just laughed and put her hat back on, switching from singing to storytelling as if they were both a part of the same conversation.

Violet paid close attention when Phoebe told stories of how different the Dukes plantation had been when she was a girl. She described a community of hundreds of slaves who made quick work of the harvest and then settled down to eat dinner together in a small city of shacks that had since been torn down.

"See that field over there, just beyond the cotton? That's where all the cabins used to be. We had dirt floors, and, in the summer, we prayed for a breeze to come through to cool us off at night. I shared mine with two other families. One of the couples had a baby boy who never stopped crying."

Phoebe told stories without missing a beat, her fingers working against the plants and reaching back into her sack automatically. But she got a faraway look in her eyes as if she was seeing the people and places she talked about.

"The baby's name was Moses, and his mother worried so much over him that her milk dried up and he nearly died."

Violet was transfixed by her grandmother's tales. At times, Rose had to nudge Violet to make her keep picking while she listened to Phoebe. Rose complained that Phoebe made slave times seem romantic.

"What happened to the baby?" Violet held her breath, not sure if this was one of Phoebe's happy-ending stories.

"Oh, the other women and I, we put her to bed and took the baby. Someone else had a newborn, too, and she had plenty of milk to share. So Moses grew plump and happy, stopped all that crying and let his mama get back to work."

Violet sighed and smiled, glad to know that even during hard times, sometimes things turned out okay.

Phoebe also spoke of beatings and deprivations, of not knowing her real mother or father, of always feeling as if she didn't belong because of her pale skin.

"I used to get regular beatings. The missus said I was getting too big for my britches, thinking I was too pretty to work," Phoebe told Violet on another day.

"But you *are* pretty," Violet said. As far as she was concerned, Phoebe, with her long, curly hair, her fawn-colored skin and her long legs, was the most beautiful woman she'd ever seen.

Rose snorted. "You don't have to tell Mama she's pretty—believe me, she knows."

Phoebe gave Rose a dark look. "I can't help the way I look, Rose, just like you can't help the way you look. And anyway, pretty is as pretty does, and I have always made a point of carrying myself well."

Violet looked back and forth between the two woman, marveling at how much they looked like sisters instead of mother and daughter.

"Anyway, Missus had other reasons for not liking me. White women never like colored girls who are too pale."

Phoebe seemed to have lost her storytelling mood and glared up at the sky. "Looks like rain. Better work faster."

Violet wanted to know more. "Why *are* you so light-skinned?" Her tactlessness was born of innocence, and she would soon learn that Negroes didn't talk about these things aloud, not even with family.

Rose swatted at her daughter, scolding her, but Phoebe shook her head.

"Can't blame her for asking, Rose. She's just a child."

"She ought to know better," Rose complained.

Violet felt a fear growing in her belly. A curious child, she asked questions all day long, exasperating her mother and making her grandmother laugh at her persistence. She wanted to know everything about the world, and without books, all she had was her own natural inquisitiveness to satisfy her need.

This was the first time she had regretted asking a question. It was the first time she regretted asking questions in the first place.

If left up to Rose, Violet's sudden wish to remain ignorant would have been granted, but Phoebe didn't believe in lying.

"My mama was sold right after I was born, and nobody ever said for sure who my daddy was."

She paused and looked back at the house, a ten-room, two-story house that sat largely empty now that the Dukes daughters had married off into other families.

Their one son, Holloway, was a year older than Phoebe and had died the year Rose was born.

Phoebe often said that they would soon be free one way or another, since the patriarch of the family was nearing eighty and his wife wasn't far behind. They could not afford to keep up the house much longer, and already they didn't have the money to pay all the sharecroppers and migrant workers needed to properly work the fields. Each year, there were fewer workers accompanying Phoebe, Rose and Violet during the harvest, and they were the only family who actually lived on-site. Phoebe had overheard talk of the farm being sold off in parcels.

"But even though it was never said, I think old Holloway Dukes was my daddy, and that's why they sent my mama away after I was born. I suppose if Junior had been married when I got Rose in my belly, they might have sent me away, too."

Violet was confused by this, and part of her wanted to ask more questions. But Rose heaved a warning sigh.

"Oh, now, Rose, the girl was bound to wonder why you and I are so fair-skinned. The only reason she came out halfway brown is because you couldn't stay away from that pretty boy who passed through here on his way to Oklahoma."

"Mama!"

The two older women began bickering, leaving Violet to ponder the identity of her own father, a man she had never known and of whom Rose refused to speak. She didn't bother to ask Rose, figuring that she could get more out of her grandmother some time when they were alone.

As much as Violet relished spending days in the fields, she relished the time she and Phoebe spent alone in their tin cabin. Rose often disappeared after dark, ignoring Violet's questions and admonishing her daughter to go to sleep and to stay out of grown folks' business. Phoebe, who always stayed up late with Violet, just shook her head and watched with sad eyes as Rose left their tiny cabin. Sometimes, Violet had the urgent feeling that Rose wasn't coming back, and once she voiced her fear to Phoebe.

"Don't worry, Violet. Rose will be back. This is her home." Her voice was, as always, low and soothing, but even six-year-old Violet could see the sorrow in Phoebe's eyes.

"Come on over, let old Phoebe braid your hair for you."

Violet loved the feeling of her grandmother's busy fingers weaving through her thick hair. Phoebe braided quickly, long, narrow braids that tamed Violet's unruly mane into swirls along her scalp and down her back.

"You're not old, Grammy."

Phoebe gave a throaty chuckle. "It might not seem so to you, little girl. But trust me, I'm old. I'm the oldest person I've ever known, and that's a fact."

Phoebe gently pushed Violet's head forward to reach the soft curls at the nape of her neck.

Violet considered this. "What about Mister Holloway? He must be 100 or so."

Phoebe threw her head back, howling with laughter, her hands shaking with mirth. Violet peeked up at her, happy to make her grandmother laugh, even if she didn't know what was so funny.

"Yes, dear Violet, you are right. Holloway Dukes is old as dirt with a personality to match. He's not quite 100, but that deal he made with the devil might just get him there."

Violet shuddered, thinking of the red-clad, forked-tail monster she had seen in a battered copy of a children's Bible. Sometimes Phoebe got used books from old Holloway Dukes, who had secretly taught Phoebe to read when she was just a little girl. Phoebe kept most of them for herself to read after Violet fell asleep at night. Rose had no interest in reading. Violet was interested in the books and reading until she came across the frightening image of the devil. Now, when she saw a book, she thought of that drooling monster and she only pretended to read to please Phoebe.

"How does Mister know the devil?"

Phoebe must have heard the panic in Violet's voice. She finished the last braid, then smoothed her hand over the girl's head, cooing and murmuring.

"Oh, baby. There isn't a real devil. At least, not like the church people talk about. I just meant that Holloway gets what he wants—always has, and as far as I can tell, always will."

Violet frowned, trying to understand what her grandmother was saying.

"So he's bad?"

Phoebe put her palms on Violet's cheeks and sighed.

"Your mother thinks you're too young to talk about these things, but you know I'll always answer any question you have. Holloway Dukes is a man who owned slaves, including your own grandmother. It's not right to own another human being, no matter what the law says."

Phoebe paused, closing her eyes for a moment. Violet waited, afraid to speak.

"But he's also your great-grandfather. It wasn't my choice, but I have always loved Rose, and I love you more than you can ever know."

Violet looked down at the floor, feeling a strange sense of shame. She didn't know many other people, just the adults she sometimes saw from nearby farms and the children of migrant workers who kept to themselves and sometimes didn't even speak English. But she knew enough to understand that being part white was a bad thing, a shameful thing.

"Who is my father?"

Phoebe's brows furrowed and her full lips narrowed into a tight line. "You'd have to ask Rose about that. Only she knows, and as far as I know, she hasn't ever told anyone."

She paused as if searching for the right words.

"Rose has always wanted more than just me for family, but that's all she's ever had. I've had twenty-six years to learn to live with what I could not control. Rose hasn't found her peace in this world, but she will. She will."

"Am I bad?" Violet's voice was a whisper. Phoebe drew her into her arms, holding her tight against her body.

"You, Violet, are a blessing. Don't ever forget that."

Half-formed questions swirled through Violet's mind as she tried to sleep on her straw mat, forming night-marish dreams throughout the night. She awoke when Rose slipped back into the cabin, more from the smell of liquor than any sound her mother made. Listening to Rose creeping around the room getting ready for bed, Violet drowsily vowed to ask Phoebe more about the family sometime soon and fell back into a troubled sleep.

But Violet never had a chance to ask Phoebe more about Holloway Dukes and his son—those white men who had white wives but also black children, who sold the cotton she spent her days picking. It was the middle of summer, and they worked hard alongside seasonal crews brought in to harvest the cotton in time. Rose still complained, Phoebe still sang and Violet still laughed, but there wasn't time for serious conversations during the days. Rose fought off exhaustion with her nighttime wanderings, but Phoebe and Violet were too tired at night to do much talking.

That fall, Phoebe got sick with influenza and died.

Rose refused to cry, even when Phoebe's body was buried in the Dukes family cemetery.

"That's the problem with loving someone. Love a person and you can be sure you'll lose them. That's how life works," she said grimly.

Violet secretly wished that her sullen mother had been taken from her instead of Phoebe.

The next summer Violet and Rose were alone in the fields and for the first time, Violet noticed how the sweat soaked through her long-sleeved shirt and long skirt before she had even made it down one row of plants. She became aware of how the rough plants scratched her hands and bare feet until they bled, how her back ached at the end of the day from all the bending and lifting. Rose sometimes yelled at Violet for being careless and getting too many tiny pieces of dirt and stems into her sack. They no longer laughed and talked to make the days go faster, both of them silently mourning the absence of Phoebe anew as they realized that she had been the one who made the 100-degree days bearable.

It was a relief when, after the harvest, the Dukes announced that the land had been sold. Rose took seven-year-old Violet east to the town of Greenville, where she had heard there were wealthy whites looking for domestic help.

"My cotton-picking days are over," Rose declared.

Violet washed and scrubbed alongside her mother, and when Rose died of tuberculosis in 1925, Violet took over her mother's jobs and was, at age sixteen, on her own.

Until she met Gray Greer.

CHAPTER 4
"I'm a Big Girl Now"

Duck
Greenville, 1942–1947

After Merline left Mother was always angry, but she never mentioned my sister's name. I was too scared to bring it up, although I wanted to ask Mother why she would leave Merline to fend for herself, why she couldn't forgive her weakness, why she was so mean and distant and hard. I took my cues from Mother and we lived quietly, with Merline like a ghost, haunting every corner of our home.

Maybe, if my mother had wanted to talk, she could have asked me questions. I knew about Kenny and Merline, knew about the baby. I knew where Merline was that very night she left, although it would take a week or so before Mother heard gossip about Merline's new job as the Banks family's maid. I was the only one who knew all the secrets. But I was Duck, and no one thought my kind of intelligence, "book-smarts," was worth much in the real world.

We were seldom in the house together. Mother still worked two jobs, and I went to school and wondered how Merline was doing. It was strange to admit to myself, but I actually missed her. Though Merline had always treated me like an annoying pest (at best) or her own personal slave (at worst), I realized that I missed having someone pay *some* kind of attention to me, even if it was negative. When Merline left, it was as if I had become invisible to Mother. When she spoke to me, her words were short, her voice flat.

Sometimes, when the nightly silence kept me up, I crept into her room to watch her sleeping. It was the only time her face relaxed and the ever-present frown lines disappeared from her forehead. My mother was pretty in the calm night, and I could see the strong resemblance between her and Merline. They shared high cheekbones, honey skin, long lashes, slim hands. At twelve years old, I already knew I looked nothing like Mother and Merline. My skin was too dark, my nose too long, my lips too full. I knew the ugly duckling in the story became a swan, graceful and lovely. I was too much of a pragmatist to hope that would ever happen to me.

These thoughts only plagued me at night. My days were occupied with school and the chores that were now all my responsibility. When Merline was bossing me around and delegating work to me, I had assumed she was shirking her own chores and passing them off to me. When she was gone, I realized that Merline had been doing a lot of work, which I now had to do or else risk looking into Mother's hard eyes while explaining why the laundry was not folded or the kitchen floor not mopped. As lonely as I was, I had no desire to rile Mother. She was like a caged animal, quiet, waiting for an excuse to attack. I would not give her that excuse.

I took care of myself. I always carried a book with me, like a shield to keep people from asking me about Merline. I lay awake nights, wondering how Merline was doing, thinking of her growing belly. Months passed, and just after I turned thirteen in June, I received a note in the mail.

"Duck, you're an auntie now," it read. "Her name is Katherine."

That was all it said. Nothing about how things were going with the Bankses, nothing about Kenny, nothing asking me how I was doing alone with Mother. But wasn't that typical of our family? Everyone kept secrets, held the truth so close it was crushed under the weight of the silence.

That night, I turned on my little plastic radio, keeping the volume low so Mother wouldn't hear it. The songs soothed me, and the voices of the men who introduced the songs were familiar and reassuring. They were old friends, reminding me that no matter what my life was like during the days, the music would always keep me company at night. When a ballad came on, the notes meandered through my mind, serenading me as I prayed.

I prayed for Merline. I prayed for Katherine. I even prayed for Mother. And I prayed for me.

A Street in Bronzeville was the first book I ever owned. Books were a luxury, and it never occurred to Mother that we might own books instead of only borrowing them from the library. Even that she found frivolous.

"If you have that much time to read, you must not be doing your chores," she complained.

But I did all the chores quickly so I could make time for the singular pleasure in my life.

Before I was seventeen, I didn't even know that black poets existed, let alone black women poets. My music teacher, Miss Lattrice, was the only other black woman I knew who liked to read just as I did. My classmates were focused on dances and boyfriends, and they ignored me because I didn't wear makeup or sew dresses meant to show off my figure. I was plain and skinny. I kept my hair in neat braids long after the other girls had begun straightening and curling their hair. Other girls my age laughed a lot and flirted with the boys. People thought I was shy and scared of boys, but I had always known that listening was more important than talking. They took home economics classes to learn to be wives and mothers who cooked, sewed and cleaned. I took music class because I wanted to learn to read music so I could write my own songs.

Miss Lattrice was the only person who didn't try to change me. She was the only person I would allow to hear me sing.

During the fall of my senior year in high school, music was my last class of the day. Most days I merely endured all the others, looking forward to the time when I could study the notes and practice them on the piano. There were only ten students in the class, and most of them were girls who knew each other from singing in the church choir. I had grown up with these girls but I didn't know any of them well. People complain about the forced intimacy of a small town, but I always thought there was nothing lonelier than being different in a small town.

While the other girls practiced hymns, Miss Lattrice let me sit at a table near the window, where I studied sheet music and daydreamed. Sometimes, when Miss Lattrice was still busy with the choir girls, I looked around at her shelves, which were filled with books and magazines I had never seen. One day, I saw an article in *Ebony Magazine* about Gwendolyn Brooks. She was from Chicago, a place that sounded foreign and cold to me. She wrote poems about being black, being plain, being poor, being lonely.

I asked Miss Lattrice about her.

"She's amazing, just amazing," she said in her formal manner of speaking. Miss Lattrice was tall and thin like me, and she had freckles all over her pale face. She wore her wavy hair pulled back into a smooth bun at the nape of her neck, and she wore square eyeglasses with black rims. She was born and raised in Greenville but left when she was fifteen. People said she had once passed as white up in New York and Chicago, but I didn't believe that. If she could pass as white, why come back to Greenville to be a black teacher in a black school?

"Gwendolyn Brooks is one of America's premier poets. You must read her," she announced, rummaging through her desk. She pulled out a dog-eared hardcover copy of *A Street in Bronzeville* and handed it to me.

"You told me you want to write your own songs. There is no better place to begin than reading poetry."

"We read Robert Frost in English class."

The assignment was to memorize "The Road Not Taken." Everyone else in the class thought the poem was dumb, too confusing, irrelevant to their lives. I quietly and secretly loved it.

Miss Lattrice cleared her throat and lowered her head to look at me over the top of her thick glasses.

"Robert Frost is certainly important. But you are a young Negro woman, like Miss Brooks. It is important to read the works of our contemporaries."

"I've never written a poem."

Miss Lattrice smiled at me. "But you have written a song, correct?"

I had never told anyone, not even Miss Lattrice, about my songs. But somehow, she knew.

"Music is poetry, Delia."

I nodded, even though I didn't quite understand what she meant.

"I'll bring the book back soon."

Miss Lattrice shook her head. "It's yours to keep. Consider it your homework: Read Miss Brook's poetry and then tell me what you think."

That night, I flipped through the pages of the book, trying to decide whether to read from the beginning or start with the first poem that caught my eye. A title jumped off the page: "Hunchback Girl, She Thinks of Heaven." I read that poem over and over. I fell asleep with the open book on my chest, and I dreamed I was the princess of properness, just like in the poem.

That winter, my mother married Rollins. She had taken a new job cleaning the local elementary school during the evenings. Rollins was the new janitor there during the days. He had moved to Greenville from Mississippi.

"I watched too many black men get lynched back home for speaking their minds. A man needs to be able to speak his mind," he declared over Sunday dinner. Mother had invited him over so he and I could "get to know each other." She even cooked—a pot roast, fried chicken and two different desserts—something she never did when it was just the two of us.

Mother beamed at him. I spooned mashed potatoes into my mouth and thought that Texas wasn't exactly a bastion of freedom for black men.

"With me, what you see is what you get," Rollins went on, looking directly at me. "I'm an honest man, doing honest work."

Rollins was a short man, standing only a couple inches taller than my mother. When he wasn't working, he liked to wear dark suits and a bright white shirt buttoned up to the top. His shoes were always shined, something my mother admired.

"I like a man who takes care with his appearance," I overheard her telling him during a rare night off.

By the time I was seventeen, we had settled into a truce: I did the chores around the house, including the cooking and shopping, and she worked as much as she could to keep a roof over our heads and food on the table. When our paths crossed, we talked about necessary arrangements, as if we were roommates rather than family. She never asked about me, about school, about the piano lessons I took with money I earned from tutoring other kids at school. She never asked if I needed anything, if I wanted anything. We never spoke of Merline.

Some nights, Mother sat alone at the kitchen table drinking from a large jug of wine and smoking. She had few friends, but sometimes one of the women she worked with would come over to gossip. I stayed in my room, listening through the air vents as I read chapters of whatever book I was reading at the time. I still knew secrets, but I cared less about other people's business and thought more about creating a life for myself.

Rollins was one of the secrets I knew about long before Mother invited him over for dinner.

"I heard he owned his own store back in Mississippi," one of Mother's friends said.

"And he had a wife and child who died in some kind of accident," she added.

"He makes a good living over at the school," my mother said.

"And, girl, he sure likes you!"

I listened, trying to pick out the sound of Mother's laughter. She laughed so rarely that when she did, it was like listening to someone speak a foreign language.

Rollins wore wire-rimmed glasses that gave him a vaguely studious look.

"I didn't get much schooling back home, but I read the newspaper every day. Keeps the mind sharp," he told my mother, who nodded in agreement.

But when she caught me reading the newspaper, she would tell me no man would ever want someone bookish like me.

At the end of the meal, Rollins smoothed his hand over his hair, which covered his head in precise waves. He brushed crumbs off his lap, touched the corners of his mouth with his napkin, and patted his round belly.

"Violet, this was the best meal I've ever had," he said, smiling.

That was the problem. His smile. All through dinner I felt unsettled, agitated in a way that made no sense. There was something off about Rollins, and I wasn't sure what it was until he smiled.

His grin was wide, showing his perfectly square teeth and the dimple in his right cheek. There was something dark in his eyes when he turned his smile on me. Something threatening, something secretive, something dangerous. A chill created tiny goose bumps on my skin. I looked away from his gaze and excused myself from the table.

When I was seventeen, my nightly dreams were filled with images of me at college. These were vivid,

Technicolor fantasies in which I could see myself in scenes as if I were watching a film. There I was, wearing a prim two-piece suit, a shoulder bag filled with books at my side, my legs crossed neatly as I took notes in a bright classroom with gleaming wooden floors. Next, I sat laughing with my classmates at a dinner table as we discussed the latest book we had read. In another scene, I sat cross-legged on a twin-sized bed, glasses perched on my noses as I studied for a big test.

The strangest thing about these dreams was my voice. College had, in my fantasies, transformed my speaking voice from low and raspy, with a slow Texas drawl, to a soprano with a clipped, almost British accent. I suppose this is how I assumed college-educated women spoke. My assumption was based solely on the speech patterns of Miss Lattrice, who had attended Howard University, had lived in Chicago for many years before returning, for reasons she never explained, to Greenville. She was the only person I knew who had attended what I considered a real college (other teachers had attended special teacher's academies or had simply volunteered for a job that few in our town would or could do). My seventeen-year-old mind assumed it was college that had shaped her way of speaking, and if I went to college, I, too, would cut my words short and change the way vowels formed on my tongue.

I wanted to go to Spelman College. I had seen a photo in *Ebony* showing the Sisters Chapel. It had a red facade set back behind six stone columns. The peaked roof looked majestic against the pearly wisps of clouds.

Mature trees were full and green, casting broad shadows over the manicured grass. I only attended church on holidays, but I could picture myself in the Sisters Chapel every Sunday, my fingers folded together underneath my chin, thanking whatever god who had allowed me to escape Greenville, Texas, and land in Atlanta, Georgia.

There would be a choir, and I would sing proudly in the way I never could at home. I would let my voice soar, find its range, fill the church with the soaring of my soul. I would finally be what I always knew I could be, a singer whose voice wasn't silenced by an indifferent mother, an absent sister, a small town that saw me only as Duck Dukes, the ugly one. I would study and become a teacher, and I would go to Sisters Chapel every week, where I would sing until my throat grew raw.

I wasn't just a dreamer. I sent away for information and applications, and my music teacher helped me fill them out. I didn't tell Mother. I knew what she would say:

"You know I don't have any money for college. I don't know where you got the idea that you should go to college, anyway. I didn't even finish high school, but I made my way. You think you're better than me? You're so busy putting on airs that you don't have any common sense. You need to get a job to support yourself, just in case you can't find a husband who'll take you."

Mother had a ready supply of reasons I shouldn't read, shouldn't dream, shouldn't try. So I kept quiet. I saved money from my tutoring. I sent out my application. And I dreamed.

The first time Rollins touched me, I told myself that it was an accident, that I was too suspicious by nature, that I was imagining things. It was January, and people said it was the warmest one they could remember in decades. Rollins had, over the past few months, become a regular fixture at Sunday dinner, and at Christmas, Mother announced they were engaged to be married.

"Rollins is a good man," she said, watching my face. It must have betrayed my doubts about his eyes. "You should be happy to have a father."

"I don't need a father," I told her. As my body had grown taller, my sprit had grown bolder. We stood in the kitchen together Christmas Eve. She was making Rollins's favorite, pecan pie. I was watching her, thinking that she had no idea what *my* favorite dessert was.

At seventeen, I towered over Mother. Where she had curves, I was thin except for breasts that continually surprised me by getting in the way of my movements. But I still wasn't up to her standards. She liked to tell me that I'd look much better if I had some meat on my bones.

Now, she looked up from shelling pecans to give me one of her frowns.

"Don't you talk to me like that."

In years past, she would have followed with the threat of a beating, but now she stopped short. I pulled back my shoulders and stood at full height. If she wanted to whip me, she would have to reach up to do it. I could see the realization in her eyes. I was no longer the child she could ignore or abuse.

She looked away from my gaze and went back to her pie.

"Everybody needs a daddy. Even smart-mouth girls need daddies."

Before I could respond, the doorbell rang. Rollins didn't wait for someone to get the door, he just walked right in, through the house and into the kitchen. I watched him with narrowed eyes as he went over and kissed Mother, then turned to me.

"How's my Darling Duck?"

He and Mother found this nickname funny, and they thought I didn't understand that calling me "darling" was a way of making fun of me. I was anything but darling when it came to Rollins and Mother. I made a point of withdrawing from them, staying in my room as much as possible, with my books for company.

"Hello, Rollins."

He glanced at Mother, who was looking at him with something close to adoration. I was seventeen, the one who was supposed to be the hopeless romantic, but my thirty-eight-year-old mother was the one who acted as if she was in puppy love.

"I suppose Violet told you that we're going to be a family. As such, I think you should stop being so formal and call me Daddy. After all, I'm going to be your father."

He stepped closer and hugged me, his arms tight around me, his hands rubbing my back in small, slow circles. It was not the type of hug a father would give a daughter. It wasn't right.

Over his shoulder, I looked at Mother. She could rescue me. She must see that he was touching me in a way that was sick, that was wrong. But she didn't see his hands on my back rubbing back and forth, up and down. She looked at me, a warning in her eyes. Don't ruin it for me, her eyes said. Don't ruin it or you'll be sorry. I looked away from her and pulled away from Rollins.

"I have reading to do," I said, and left the room before anyone could answer.

He gave me a sweater for a Christmas present, and Mother made me try it on. As thin as I was, it was too tight, and I watched him watching me as I modeled it with hunched shoulders. When Mother's attention was elsewhere, he grinned at me.

In April, I started watching the mail, waiting for a letter from Spelman. That spring I was filled with excitement and dread. During the days, I was thrilled by my growing savings and the prospect of actually going to college. If I could just save $500, it would be enough to get me to Atlanta by bus, enough to keep me fed through the first year at Spelman. I would figure out the rest once I got there.

But at night, my fantastic college dreams had turned to nightmares about rejection from Spelman, being trapped in Greenville for the rest of my life, doomed to repeat the life I saw all around me. As the deadline neared, I felt torn, with hope and dejection pulling me in opposite directions.

One night, my dream-self opened a letter from Spelman. The paper felt heavy in my hands, almost like cloth, and it was the color of freshly churned butter. It was just a single page document, filled with small, typed letters from one edge to the other. There was no signature, no salutation, just long sentences and paragraphs. In the middle of the page, a photo of the Sisters Chapel in bright colors had text flowing around it. The words described all the ways in which I was not Spelman material. I was too ugly, too poor, too tall, too dumb, and most of all, my name was ridiculous. No one called Duck would ever be a Spelman woman. I would be an embarrassment to Spelman, and a girl like me had a lot of nerve even applying to college, let alone imagining that I would get in.

I wanted to cry but I couldn't find my voice. My vocal cords were gone and my throat hurt from trying to scream out that I was good enough for Spelman, that my name was Delia, not Duck. Then the buttery paper started to make my hands sting, and I dropped it to look at my palms. They were blistering before my eyes and suddenly I was able to scream that I was poisoned, poisoned, poisoned. I could smell my hands as I watched the skin peel away from the muscles underneath, and the room filled with the sickly sweet, vaguely familiar odor of Juicy Fruit gum and coconut hair grease.

I woke slowly, my dream-self still baffled by poison that smelled so odd and so familiar, my real self gradually realizing it had been a dream. My pillow was wet with my tears, and I took deep breaths while my eyes adjusted to the darkness and the objects in my room came into shadowed focus. The horror faded, and the dream started to seem silly and unrealistic. My eyes rested on an unfamiliar shape standing next to the door. I sat up and realized that one thing from my dream remained: the smell.

The shape moved toward me, gradually turning into a person, then a man. The smell intensified, and I suddenly knew why it was familiar. Rollins.

By that time, he was standing next to my bed, towering over me like a monster in the dark, and just as I opened my mouth to order him out of my room, he threw all of his weight on top of me. The air rushed out of me, and we were still for a brief moment. In that moment, the only sound in the room was the rasp of his panting. Then he pinned my limbs down with his and propped himself up over me, grinning.

"Why aren't you screaming?"

It had never occurred to me to scream. I was so used to taking care of myself that I never even considered that Mother could rescue me. I was only seventeen, but I already felt alone in the world.

"Get off me." I tried to move my arms and legs, but he was too strong.

"You know why you didn't scream? Because you want this. I can tell by the way you watch me. Now, I'm going to give you what you want."

He pushed his face toward mine, and the smell of the gum he was still chewing made me want to gag. Instead, I bashed my forehead into his and when he cried out and loosened his grip on my arms and legs, I brought up both knees into his crotch. He gave a girlish shriek and fell onto the floor, curled over in pain. I huddled into the far corner and watched him as he crawled out of my room, still whimpering in pain, a large knot already swelling on his forehead.

I shut the door behind him and dragged my dresser in front of it. I slid to the floor and sat with my back against the lowest drawer, waiting for my pulse to slow. I must have dozed off, but I was jolted awake by the sounds of Rollins getting ready for work in the bathroom. He left for work earlier than Mother, so I knew she would still be in bed when he left the house. I waited for the bang of the screen door closing and the clop of his footsteps on the road in front of our house. My window was open and I could hear him whistling, as if he didn't have a care in the world. I waited for his whistle to fade into silence before I moved the furniture back and opened my door.

I waited for Mother in the kitchen. I had spent the past thirty minutes trying to find ways to make her believe me, to show her that Rollins was evil, to ask her to protect me.

She spoke first after pouring herself a cup of coffee. "I heard you scream last night. You've been having a lot of dreams lately. Too much reading, probably. Gets your imagination going and the next thing you know, you're keeping the whole house awake at night."

I took a deep breath. "That wasn't me. It was Rollins."

She looked at me and rolled her eyes. "Rollins was in the bed next to me." She looked at me with something like motherly concern, a rare interest.

"You have dark circles under your eyes. You need to get more sleep, stop all that dreaming."

It was always my fault. Anything that was wrong was because of something I did. This is the way it had always been. I couldn't explain my dreams to her because she had no idea I had applied to Spelman, no idea how worried I was about not getting in. So I told her the truth.

"Rollins came into my room last night and I hit him. That's why he screamed."

Mother watched my face, and for a moment, I thought she believed me. Maybe, for the first time, she would protect me. Maybe I had been wrong about her.

Then she turned to the refrigerator to get milk for her coffee.

"Now I know you were dreaming," she said over her shoulder. "Rollins has no reason to be in your bedroom at night."

She refilled her cup, and without another glance my way, went to get dressed for the day. After a long while, I got up and went to school.

I had two choices.

Choice 1: I could stay and finish high school, counting on the possibility that the real letter from

Spelman would welcome me to Atlanta, hoping that Rollins would be scared off by the fact that I had told Mother, even though she hadn't believed me. Maybe if I told Miss Lattrice, she could help. I could keep saving my tutoring money and earn the $500 I needed to get to Spelman and survive for a few months. I could live my life believing that everything was going to work out.

Choice 2: If I told Miss Lattrice, she might not believe me, either. No one talked about these kinds of things, and all I could think of was how dirty I felt. I didn't want Miss Lattrice to think I was trash. I wanted her to think of me as a musician, as a student, not as a girl to be pitied. And Rollins wasn't going to stop until he got what he wanted. College or not, I could not live with that. I would have done almost anything for the chance to go to Spelman. Almost.

April 10, 1947, was a crisp, sunny Thursday in Greenville. Some years, it was already as hot as July by that time of year, and I would feel as if spring were a short pit stop between winter and summer. But that year, April had been cooler than normal, with breezes that smelled like the ocean to me, even though we weren't near any water at all. Walking home from school that day, I took special notice of how bright green the new leaves on the trees were, how the sky was a cloudless cerulean that looked almost artificial in its clarity. I took off my jacket and tied the sleeves around my waist, letting the sun warm my face, neck, and arms. I breathed in the scent of the rosebuds and tulips some people planted near their front porches and doors.

As usual, the house was empty when I got home from school. As I had every day for two weeks, I checked the mailbox. Today, there was a large envelope from Spelman College.

I paused on the porch, letting my fingers run over the envelope. Buttery, smooth, just as it was in my dreams. I held the envelope up to my nose and there was no odor at all. I looked out at the road from Mother's front porch and I paused, feeling optimistic. I looked back at the front door, remembering the heaviness of Rollins's body on top of mine.

I did not open the envelope.

Inside, I went straight to my room. I took out my money from my secret place underneath the bed and counted it. I had $217.47. I found an old suitcase in the hall closet and packed clothes into it. I stuffed my radio into the case, using layers of clothing to cushion it. I wanted to bring my music books with me, but they were too large and they belonged to the school. I hoped that some other girl would fall in love with music the same way I had. Maybe she would be more of an optimist than I was. Maybe she would get to go to Spelman College.

No matter what the letter said, I knew I wasn't going to Atlanta. I couldn't stay and finish high school. I couldn't risk letting Rollins finish what he had started. I was leaving, but I wasn't sure where I was going until my eyes fell on my copy of Gwendolyn Brooks' *A Street in Bronzeville*. She was from Chicago. Miss Lattrice had lived there. That was where I was going. Chicago.

The book of poems was the last thing I packed. I hurried from the house without looking back. Merline and Kenny were optimists, and look where it had gotten them. I was a realist, a survivor. I was leaving Greenville behind.

CHAPTER 5

"The Lonesome Road"

Merline
Greenville, 1947

She sat outside taking a rare break, watching Katherine play with her dolls underneath an old white ash tree that she loved because it turned pink and purple in the fall.

"Pink and purple is my favorite colors," Katherine had announced one afternoon not long after she turned five.

"Pink and purple *are* my favorite colors," Mrs. Banks had told her firmly. Merline had not realized the older woman was in the room. This is what she did while Merline performed all the chores around the house: skulk around watching Katherine all day, butting in to correct what Katherine said or did before Merline even had a chance to open her mouth. Merline hated the greedy look in the woman's eyes when she watched Katherine. It was as if she wanted to devour the little girl. Her eyes glistened with need, and it worried Merline.

But then again, she thought, watching her daughter, who wouldn't want to watch little Katherine all day? The girl was five and already she was luminous. Her blonde hair curled down her back in ringlets. Deep dimples appeared in both cheeks when she smiled, which was often. And her large, hazel eyes—the only part of her that resembled Merline—twinkled with kindness for everyone and everything she came across. Katherine loved Mrs. Banks and merely giggled when the old woman corrected her grammar. She loved Mr. Banks, who never smiled, but read to Katherine every night after dinner "to educate her properly so she might turn out to be more than a washwoman like her mother."

Most of all, she loved her mother. Where Merline went, Katherine was never far behind. She watched her mother work, singing songs while Merline folded clothes, offering to help when Merline planted yellow daisies outside the window of the small room they shared. Katherine made up fairy tales to match the ones Mr. Banks read her in the evenings, and made Merline laugh with her silly names and absurd plot twists. Merline wanted to tell Katherine that her Aunt Duck loved stories, too, but she never spoke about her family.

"Where did you come from, Mama?" Katherine often asked.

"Greenville, same as you."

"But *where* did you live?"

"Oh, far away," Merline would answer, waving her hand vaguely.

"Do we have family there? Can we visit them?"

This was the only thing that could put shadows in Katherine's eyes. Like other only children, she was adept at entertaining herself, but she longed for playmates just the same. There were no other children in the house, and they seldom left the safety of their vast property. Merline thought that the only way she could protect Katherine was to keep her here, protected from gossip and curiosity. The outside world represented danger. So Katherine didn't have any playmates. It was better that way.

"Oh, maybe someday we can visit my family," Merline lied. "Now, finish telling me about Princess Kitty-Kat and her castle made of sand."

Merline used distraction and avoidance to keep Katherine from asking too many questions about Mother and Duck. She had not seen either of them since Mother kicked her out of their small house five years ago.

That's why Merline's mouth fell wide open on that fine April day when Duck walked up to the yard through the back woods. Merline looked from side to side quickly before rushing up to Duck. Two feet from her sister, she stopped short.

Merline couldn't believe how much her sister had changed. She remembered Duck as an awkward twelve-year-old with bony limbs and a big nose. Somehow, Duck had grown into her features and was now tall and slender but not skinny. She wore simple clothing and no makeup, and there was a natural loveliness that shone from her prominent cheekbones and her full lips. She even walked differently, her head up, shoulders back instead of slouched. The only thing childlike about her was her hair, which was done in two braids. Duck carried a small suitcase, a determined look on her face.

Merline felt a knot of jealousy grow in her throat. Duck was going somewhere. She was free. Merline glanced over at Katherine, feeling a rare resentment. Duck's life was open to possibility. Merline was living her future, and the possibilities were limited.

The sisters stood silent, staring at each other. Merline had no idea what to say, how to breach the five years between them.

"I'm leaving," Duck said. "I came to say goodbye."

Merline was ashamed. She knew that she would not have done the same for Duck, that if she had a chance to escape, if things had gone differently for her, she wouldn't have thought twice about leaving her sister behind. Hadn't she done just that when she had gone to work for the Banks family? She hadn't seen or spoken to her family in five years.

Merline wanted to tell this new version of her sister that she was sorry for bossing her around when they were children, sorry for telling her she was ugly. Sorry for not being a big sister in the most important ways. But Merline wasn't used to apologizing, and the words stuck in her throat.

"Why now? I always figured you would finish high school, maybe go to one of those colleges for Negroes."

Duck took her time answering. "Mother got married again. There wasn't room for all of us."

Merline started to question this, but the look on Duck's face discouraged further discussion.

"Where are you going?"

"Chicago."

Merline tried to imagine Chicago, but she couldn't fix an image in her mind. All she could think of was Duck, alone, in a strange city among people with strange accents.

"Mommy, who is this?" Katherine asked, tugging on Merline's skirt. Merline watched as Duck looked down at Katherine, then up at Merline.

Merline squatted down next to her daughter. "Katherine, this is your Aunt Duck."

The sound of Katherine giggles rang through the air. "Your name is Duck? What a silly name!"

Duck smiled and held out her hand to Katherine. "Isn't it? You'd think I would quack instead of talk, right?"

Katherine laughed again. "Quack, quack!"

Merline watched while her sister and daughter chattered about ducks and names. She liked seeing Katherine happy, and Duck was good with her. Merline let herself imagine how different things could have been if Duck and Katherine could have gotten to know each other.

"Duck is going to Chicago," Merline blurted. She wanted to cut things short before Katherine developed too much interest in Duck. It would be difficult to explain why she couldn't see her aunt on a regular basis.

Duck and Katherine turned to look at her.

"What's Chicago?"

"A big city in the North, right on a lake. People wear big coats and boots there, and they talk funny. Like this," Duck said, making Katherine giggle with her imitation of a Northern accent.

"Mama, can we go to Chicago to visit Aunt Duck?"

Merline wanted to say yes, wanted to go grab a suitcase and follow Duck right out of town. But she couldn't. She wouldn't. She looked at her fair-skinned, blonde-haired daughter and shook her head.

"We belong here."

Duck suddenly hugged Merline, and then she reached down to hug Katherine. She whispered something into the little girl's ear.

"My bus leaves soon," Duck said. She picked up her bag and took one last look at Katherine before meeting Merline's eyes.

Merline nodded. "Take care of yourself."

Duck held Merline's gaze for a moment, then turned away. Katherine went back to playing with her dolls, and after a long while, Merline went back to her chores.

When Katherine was born, Merline couldn't believe how pale and fragile she looked, like a just-hatched chick without even a bit of fluff to protect her translucent skin. She even cried like fowl, her screams more like squawking than anything else. She had a head full of curly blonde hair. Just like her father, is what Merline thought when the nurse handed her the baby.

"You know you can give her up for adoption. There are a lot of families out West who won't ask about the parents of a baby who looks like this," the nurse told Merline. She was not much older than Merline, with dark hair pulled back into a severe bun underneath her nurse's cap. She was the only one who smiled at Merline, the only one who didn't treat her as if she had something to be ashamed of. After Merline woke up, that nice nurse had brought her hard candy and extra water to help her shake off the medicine they'd given her to knock her out during the birth.

Merline looked down at the tiny bundle in her arms, then up at the nurse's bosom, which strained against her tight uniform.

"This is my daughter. I am going to keep her."

She did not meet the nurse's gaze, which made her feel even worse than the labor pains or the aching between her legs. The young woman seemed nice, but her eyes were filled with pity. Merline did not want anyone's pity.

"But the baby . . . she looks like her father, right? That's not going to be easy." The nurse spoke softly, her voice drenched with sympathy.

Merline looked closely at the woman. She noticed her skin that had a tint of gold and the hair that looked like it might be just a touch kinky if it wasn't brushed back so tightly. She looked at the nametag pinned to her white dress. Nurse Lovell.

"I know how hard it will be," Nurse Lovell whispered, leaning close and stroking the baby's hair. "Sometimes I wish my mama had done for me what you can do for this poor little girl."

When she whispered these last words, her accent changed from clipped and educated to soft and drawling. She was a Negro, just like Merline. Except she wasn't. She was a white nurse working in the Negro section of the hospital, telling Merline she should give her baby away.

"Where's your mama now?"

Nurse Lovell stood up straight and looked away, her jaw clenched.

"I haven't seen her in a long time."

She became busy then, checking Merline's chart and flipping the pages so quickly that she couldn't have read a word. "You think about what I said. Your daughter will be much better off."

Merline held Katherine close to her for a long while after the nurse left. She loathed the nurse for what she'd said, partly because she suspected the woman was right. It was likely that Katherine might be better off without her. She could not imagine what Nurse Lovell's life had been like, keeping that kind of secret, always worrying that someone would find out she was not what she claimed to be. Then again, Merline had a secret, too. If she wanted to keep her job, keep a roof over her head, live in the house where Kenny grew up, she could never tell anyone who Katherine's real father was. But the fact that Kenny might come home, would surely come home eventually, was enough to get Merline through the days. That hope and this baby were all Merline had. What would Kenny think when he finally came home and the baby was gone?

There was no way she was giving her baby away.

No matter how much she yearned to escape, Merline would never leave the Banks home. Not when there was a chance Kenny would come back to see his daughter. Not when there was a chance Kenny would come back to see Merline.

CHAPTER 6

"Singin' the Blues"

Violet
1925–1927

Violet first saw Grayson Greer while she was working one sunny January afternoon. She was using vinegar and water to clean the kitchen windows of a large home whose owners were having an extra bedroom added on to the back of their home to accommodate their fifth child. She was only sixteen, but she looked older, having worked nearly her entire life. An only child born to an only child, she thought that one baby was plenty and five seemed greedy and foolish. Her grandmother, Phoebe, had believed that every child was a blessing, but Violet had come to agree with her mother, Rose, who had always said that loving another person just meant you had something to lose later down the line. Having lost both Phoebe and Rose, Violet didn't relish any more loss in her life.

It wasn't that she had a plan for her life. She just took one day at a time, making enough money for food, clothing and a rented room at a boarding house owned by an old colored woman who stayed out of her tenants' lives and didn't care why a sixteen-year-old girl from the high plains of Texas was now living on her own in Greenville.

So she washed the windows and watched the workers, colored and Mexican boys, sawing, pounding and nailing in preparation for the new baby. The men ignored her as they kept moving to fight off the January chill. Most of them wore gloves and hats drawn down low over their brows, but there was one who was bareheaded while he worked and joked with the others. He was very tall and his shoulders were broad and strong in his lightweight jacket. He wore jeans and boots like the others, and Violet noticed there was a paperback book stuffed in the back pocket of his pants. One of the other workers said something, and the hatless man threw his head back and laughed, a joyful sound that made her smile. She leaned closer to the window, straining to hear what he said in reply.

"You boys don't know winter. You're freezing out here, Billy over there with a scarf around his neck, Ramon whining about his numb hands. I'm from Philadelphia. There we have a real winter. In January, we've got snow coming from above, ice below our feet and a cold wind that makes your eyes water."

His accent was strange, clipped and a bit nasal, unlike the slow drawl of native Texans or the lyrical Spanish accent of the Mexican workers. Violet heard the other men's voices rise in a chorus of complaints.

"This is the coldest winter ever!"

"I slept by the fire just so I wouldn't die and leave my mama all alone!"

"*Amigo*, I am from Mexico—*no me gusta el frio.*"

The hatless man waved a hand at them and picked up a hammer. "I'm just saying, you all don't know what cold really is. This," he said, looking up at the sky, down at the ground, then licking his finger and holding it in the air, "this is like spring back in Philly."

Then he pointed at one young man in the crowd who looked about Violet's age and wore a crimson hand-knitted hat with a pom-pom on top. "And a real man, if he *must* wear a hat, should not, I repeat, should NOT, wear a hat his mama made for him."

The men broke into laughter and returned to their tasks. Violet giggled softly, and the hatless man looked up at her as if he had heard her laughter through the window. They looked at each other for a long moment. Violet looked down at her hands, embarrassed to be caught eavesdropping. When she looked up again, thinking the man would have gone back to work, she saw that he was still watching her. His smile had spread into a lazy grin, deepening the dimple in his left cheek. His hair was shorn close to his head, and his honey-colored skin seemed to glow in the late-afternoon sunlight. He was what Phoebe would have called a pretty man, the kind of man Rose would have derided as a half-breed despite her own mixed heritage. Violet noticed that he was the only light-skinned man in the group, and she wondered where he had come from.

He waved to her and she hid her smile, going back to wiping the window with an old newspaper. She didn't look back outside, moving on to other tasks. That evening, the man with no hat and the funny accent was standing at the end of the driveway in the darkness, smoking a cigarette, waiting. He smiled at her as if they had known each other all their lives, and Violet couldn't help but smile back.

"My name is Grayson Greer. People call me Gray. I'd be honored if you'd let me walk you home. It's not right for a lady to have to find her way in the dark."

She pulled her coat tightly around her shoulders. She had learned from Rose how to take care of herself. She didn't ask anyone for anything, she paid her own way and she did not allow herself to be sweet-talked by men who, as Rose put it, were "looking to have a little bit of fun before they left a woman behind with a baby in her belly."

But Phoebe had taught Violet to think for herself, and what she thought right now is that she liked the way he could still smile even after a long day's work. She liked the way his northern accent made common words sound foreign and exotic to her ears. She simply liked Grayson Greer. Gray.

"I'm Violet Dukes."

"Violet." He paused as if savoring a sweet taste on his tongue. "I once had a violet scone dipped in violet syrup when I was in France, during the war. It was the sweetest thing I've ever had in my life."

He held out his arm and together they walked down the road, talking.

World War I veteran Gray Greer returned to Philadelphia when he was eighteen, feeling older than the oldest men he saw shuffling around the neighborhood. He was filled with regrets. He regretted lying about his age to enlist, he regretted fighting a war to protect a country where he was treated worse than he had been in foreign lands. On most days, he regretted coming back to Philadelphia altogether. He had never lived anywhere else in America, but he had an intimate knowledge of certain parts of England, France and Belgium. He regretted that his life felt as if it was over, as if his best years had passed before he understood anything about life itself.

Gray had not seen any battle time. He was assigned to a labor battalion, where he was assigned menial tasks and harassed by white soldiers, who used the Negro soldiers as a outlet for their pent-up frustrations. Gray had volunteered for the Army, thinking that fighting for America might make him a man, might serve as a way to prove to the world that he was a man. But at the Army posts in France, his fellow American soldiers called him "boy" and ignored the surprised expressions of the French soldiers. The Frenchmen had their own prejudices, but they were less about skin color and more about religion, class, and culture.

"Why do you they treat you like the enemy?" a Frenchman named Georges once asked Gray. He spoke English well, though with a heavy accent it took Gray time to decipher. They were working together at one of the makeshift jail buildings where the Allied forces kept extra equipment and, sometimes, prisoners. They wore the same drab khaki pants with white T-shirts and olive green jackets that did little to fight off the chill in the cells they cleaned. Georges worked with an unlit cigarette handing from the corner of his mouth.

Gray shrugged, swiping at the floor with his mop.

"That's how white people treat colored people back home."

Georges had been sponging down the cinder-block walls but he stopped and looked up at Gray.

"But you are all Americans. It does not make sense. Why does the skin color matter?"

Gray, already weary and homesick after just a year at war, smiled grimly.

"Sometimes in America, skin color is the *only* thing that matters."

He took the cigarette Georges offered and lit it. "Where I was born, down in Texas, there are signs telling colored folks where they're allowed to go and where they're not allowed to go. Now the place I grew up, Philadelphia, Pennsylvania, there aren't any signs. You just know."

Georges shook his head, mystified. "You Americans, you worry about the wrong things. You have heard of Karl Marx? No? He is a smart man. He says the problems between men are all about rich against poor. This war, all wars, they are about money, class. If we shared the money, divided it equally, things would be better. I would be back in my village romancing a sweet girl." Georges grinned and signaled that they should take a break.

The two men sat down on a rickety wooden bench, their mops and rags forgotten. Gray lit a new cigarette from his first and offered Georges a match.

"Rich and poor, huh? Well, I don't know any rich colored people, and no white man I knew ever shared so much as a dime with a colored man, so I don't see how Mr. Marx can help us out any."

Georges looked around the room, then he pulled a well-worn paperback book from his jacket pocket. It was titled *Manifeste Communiste* by Karl Marx. The cover was stark black with white lettering, and the cover was battered and creased as if it had been read many times. Georges held the book gently in his hands, as if it were sacred. Gray remembered seeing his own mother hold her Bible in much the same way.

"This book, it explains how we, the proletarians, can overcome the bourgeoisie. We will finally have the power to control our own lives, our destinies."

Gray was just seventeen years old. He had attended school until he was fifteen and had to work to support himself when his mother and father died of influenza. He had always been a reader and had gotten straight A's in school until he dropped out. But the words Georges spoke sounded foreign and mysterious, even though Georges spoke English quite well. He listened as Georges further explained the book, speaking of *instruments of production, monopoly,* and *revolution.*

"So in America, would the white people be the bourgeoisie?"

Georges slapped the cover of the book. "Yes! And the coloreds are the proletarians. So, you see, the words of Karl Marx can work for you, too."

Gray took a long drag and finished his cigarette, stubbing it under his boot. "I'm just one man. What can I do to change things? You saw how the whites treat us. You think Karl Marx can change things?"

Georges shrugged. He pinched the end of his own cigarette and placed the remainder in his back pocket for later. *Manifeste Communiste* went back into his jacket.

"How can you know if you don't try?" He picked up his rags and bucket and moved back to the wall he had been scrubbing.

The next year, the war was over. Georges went home first—to his village near Calais. He startled Gray by hugging him goodbye. It was the first time a white man had ever touched Gray, let alone shown him affection.

"You will take care of yourself back in your home, Philadelphia?"

Gray smiled and thanked him. "Watch out for those pretty girls back home, Georges."

Georges saluted him and turned to leave. "Perhaps we will meet again, comrade."

"What does 'comrade' mean?" Gray called to Georges as he reached the door.

Georges turned and grinned. "A comrade is a friend. Goodbye, my friend."

Gray turned to zip up his own duffle bag and spotted an unfamiliar object. He pulled out a small book. *The Manifesto of the Communist Party.* There was an inscription on the inside cover, written in straight, lean script: "Revolution can be a grand affair, or it can be a small moment. I hope you find your moments back home in America. Your comrade, Georges."

Philadelphia was changing when Gray returned from the war. Because so many young white men had been killed in the war, there were many jobs for black men like Gray. These were men who had either served as laborers overseas or had not gone to fight for a war that few understood. This was a good thing for Gray. He found steady work in a paper factory and rented a small apartment, where he led a Spartan existence. He worked long hours, not for the money, but to avoid having too much leisure time to think. Thinking, he had discovered, only led to more of the empty feeling that he had come to dread since his return from France. He had no family, no friends except his co-workers, but there was little time to socialize while working. Gray preferred to spend his breaks off on his own, taking a walk or smoking around the back of the hulking gray factory building. Occasionally, he shared his bed with a woman, but he always made sure to end things before attachments could form.

The one thing he did was read. His own copy of the *Communist Manifesto* had become as creased as Georges's, and he got a library card to access thousands of books that introduced him to ideas and people he'd never known existed. He read during his lunch break, he read before falling into a dreamless sleep every night. On weekends when there was no overtime work, he spent hours lying on his scratchy, brown sofa, reading.

Early on Gray dismissed Karl Marx as an idealist whose ideas, while interesting, had nothing to do with Philadelphia in 1918. He tried reading other nonfiction, but he soon realized that he preferred fiction. Novels offered an escape from the factory, from the grumbling of white workers who resented the black faces that filled the jobs of dead white soldiers. Stories shielded Gray from the restlessness of the colored leaders, whose voices were growing louder, demanding to be called Negro, asking for equality and joining the NAACP. Gray read Burroughs, Cather, Poe and Hawthorne. He liked Twain and Dickens, avoided poetry altogether, and considered James overrated. He finished James Weldon Johnson's *Autobiography of an Ex-Coloured Man*, though it drew his attention too closely to the racial tensions that plagued cities around the country, including Philadelphia.

Gray might have gone on this way forever, reading and escaping, except that in 1925, three things happened in quick succession: A fire gutted the paper factory, his landlord told him in subtle language that blacks were no longer welcome to rent, and Gray fell in love. Left with no job, no home, and the helplessness of love, he bought a bus ticket and headed west, unsure where he was going and unaware that his journey would end in Greenville, Texas.

Gray and Violet were married two months from the day they met, and seven months after that, their baby girl was born. They named her Merline Phoebe Greer after Grayson's mother and Violet's grandmother.

Gray built them a small cabin on an abandoned patch of land where a few other Negroes lived, and Violet sewed curtains and bedspreads while the baby napped. When Gray came home from his construction jobs, the first thing he did was kiss Violet long and hard. Then he took the glass of lemonade Violet handed him, cradled the baby in his arms and sat down at the table to talk to Violet. They had started talking that first night, and it seemed to Violet that they hadn't stopped since. Violet told Gray all about her family, about picking cotton at the Dukes farm. She remembered Phoebe's stories and retold them, loving the sound of Gray's laughter. Gray told Violet about the war, about Georges, about Philadelphia, a place she'd never even heard of until the day she met Gray. She liked to sit and listen to him talk, and it seemed to Violet that Gray knew a little bit about everything.

"It's because I read. I might not be educated like all those fancy-dressing Negroes like Langston Hughes and W.E.B. DuBois, but I have learned a lot about the world by reading," he told her one night when Merline was just a few months old.

Violet made a face, remembering the illustrated Bible with the red devil-monster she'd dreamed of as a child. She still didn't like to read and preferred to listen to music on the radio when she wasn't working.

"So that's where you get all those troublemaking ideas of yours," she teased. He had told her all about the NAACP and a man named Karl Marx, who, as far as she could tell, used big words and didn't seem to understand the natural order of the world.

"Want to be treated like a man isn't making trouble. Why is it so wrong to want respect?"

This was an ongoing discussion between them. Violet believed it was best to stay as far away from whites as possible. We coloreds—she stopped and corrected herself when she noticed Gray's frown. He insisted that she say "Negroes" instead of "colored."

"We *Negroes* always end up on the wrong side when we go up against them. That's how it always been and how it will always be," she said with a shrug.

Gray shook his head. "If you read *Souls of Black Folk*," you would change your mind."

Since leaving Philadelphia, he had changed his policy of ignoring current events in favor of fiction. He still read novels, but living in Texas, he saw the stark consequences of inequality in ways that weren't apparent in Philadelphia. Jim Crow had his people in a stranglehold, and he remembered what Georges had said about revolution. Gray was looking for his small moment, and against Violet's wishes he had joined the Dallas branch of the NAACP.

"I don't need to read to find the truth. All I need to do is look around little old Greenville to know that white folks aren't going to give an inch."

"But how will we know if we don't even try?"

Violet looked down at Merline, who had finished feeding at her breast and was now sleeping with her pink lips pursed as if she was drinking milk in her dreams. She was amazed at how pale Merline was, looking more like Phoebe and Rose than Violet, whose skin was a deep russet brown.

"Gray, we've got a baby to think about. Stirring up trouble won't be good for Merline. What if something happened to you? To me? She needs us, and if being good parents means that we set all that civil rights business aside, then it's what we have to do."

She got up slowly to avoid waking the baby. Violet leaned over and kissed Gray's cheek before she left to put Merline down in the bassinet Gray had built from wood scraps.

Later, after they had gone to bed, it occurred to her that although Gray had listened to what she said about staying out of race issues, he hadn't *agreed* with her.

"Gray, are you awake?" she whispered into the darkness. He didn't reply. She listened to the rhythm of his breathing for a long while until she fell into a troubled sleep.

In 1927, when Violet was eighteen and Merline was two years old, Gray began to travel for work, looking for construction and labor jobs around the state.

"We need to save for Merline's schooling, college," he said.

Violet shook her head at the idea of a black girl going to college, but she loved Gray too much to keep him from dreaming. He was an optimist, always smiling even when he had plenty of cause not to. She sometimes allowed herself to dream with him. Some days, Gray's sunny disposition made her think that Rose had it all wrong, that loving someone could bring more happiness than grief. Merline had her father's dimples and wide-mouthed smile, and Violet wanted more than anything for her daughter to live in the kind of world that Gray thought was possible.

So he went off to make extra money for Merline's future, and Violet didn't object, even though she was lonely with just a toddler and her radio to keep her company. He was usually gone for one or two weeks at a time, and she didn't even complain when he had to be away on Thanksgiving, because he'd promised to come home in time for Christmas. He wrote her every day and sometimes his letters reached her after he was already home, and they laughingly read them together, snuggled next to each other in bed, Merline asleep in the next room.

Gray was due home from a job in Houston on Friday, December 16, 1927. When he didn't show up at the door by midnight, Violet told herself that he had probably missed his bus. The next day, she told herself that the job had gone longer and that Gray had taken the extra work to pad their savings, maybe to buy extra Christmas gifts. On Sunday she dressed Merline in her prettiest dress, blue velvet trimmed in white lace, put on her rarely used stockings and heels and went to Second Baptist Church, a place where she had been only once before. Violet and Gray put little stock in formal religion, but he had dragged her to a church dinner where he was due to meet a couple of men who'd expressed hesitant interest in the NAACP.

But when he was two days late coming home, Violet decided it wouldn't hurt to pray.

On Monday morning, a Negro man wearing a navy blue suit, a crisp white shirt, and round, wire-rimmed glasses knocked on her door. Violet had watched the stranger coming up the road from her front window, where she had stationed herself before dawn. She had told herself that she was waiting for Gray, but when the stranger approached her door, she realized that some part of her had expected this man instead.

There had been an anti-lynching rally outside of Houston on Thursday morning. Gray went to the demonstration, thinking he would take a late bus and get home early Friday. A rowdy group of white men, suspected members of the Klan, were there to heckle. Gray had been vocal, and he was involved in a brief scuffle before the police broke up the rally. The stranger shook Gray's hand and bid him safe travel.

Friday morning Gray's body was found hanging from a tree in front of the Houston church where the NAACP held its meetings.

Violet could not remember what she said to the stranger. She had a vague memory of several women from the neighborhood moving around the kitchen, talking in low voices and glancing over at Violet, who remained in her post at the window.

Later, having been moved into her bed, she dreamed of Rose. Rose was talking to her, wagging a finger in her face.

"That's the problem with loving someone. Love a person and you can be sure you'll lose them," her dream mother reminded her. "That's how life works."

CHAPTER 7
"At Last"

Duck
Chicago, 1950

I looked out at the empty room. Chairs were stacked upside down on round tables. No smoke wafted toward the ceiling, and the room smelled of the bleach I used to clean the floors. The overhead lights, used only while I did my cleaning, shone too yellow. During the day, this place was nothing special, just a large room with worn red carpet and water spots on the back walls.

I imagined the clinking of glassware, the low murmurs of an audience that wasn't there. I pictured myself standing off-stage in a low-cut silver gown, its full skirt swishing around my knees. My hair was long and straight, piled high on my head, curls strategically arranged around my face. I closed my eyes and heard the tinkle of the piano keys as the band warmed up. The master of ceremonies stepped to the single microphone standing the center of the stage. He wore a tuxedo, and his hair was waved and brushed back neatly from his forehead. Only his full lips and café au lait skin hinted at his African ancestors. The spotlight illuminated his precise mustache and practiced smile as he held up two hands to silence the audience, who obediently waited, leaning slightly forward in anticipation.

"And now . . . tonight's featured performer . . . Delia Dukes!"

The applause drowned out his booming voice before he finished saying my last name. I stepped out onto the stage and the audience stood, clapping enthusiastically until I uttered a low "thank you" into the mike. I closed my eyes, and this was the cue. My audience sat. I took a deep breath and let out the first notes, the two words, drawn out impossibly long, with a low urgency. It was as if I was singing these words for the first time, feeling each syllable. I began with this song every night. Every man in the place felt as if I was singing to him. Every woman felt as if I had read her thoughts and was singing on her behalf. No one knew better than me how it felt to find true love. No one could express this relief, this joy, this keen pleasure better than I could. No one.

"At last . . ."

The first words were like a sentence unto themselves. After I sang them, I let the silence hang in the air for a moment before signaling the band to begin, before continuing my song.

". . . My love has come along. My lonely days are over, and life is like a song."

It was a short song, not even three minutes long, but I made it last a lifetime of hope and passion. The silver dress shimmered over my swaying hips, and my red lips curved sweetly around every word. I was the queen of this stage, this night, this world. I felt every note and made each person listening feel, too. They adored me, and that adoration washed away every hurt I had ever known. In turn, I gave everything to my audience, and when the song was finished, everyone in the room felt regret. I acknowledged the raucous applause with a smile, letting it echo through the room before it died naturally and it was time for my next number.

When I opened my eyes, it was daytime at the Royale Ballroom. I was holding my broom, wearing a scarf over my hair, an old pair of blue jeans and a long-sleeved button-down shirt. I was covered in grime and dust, and no one knew me as Delia, just twenty-year-old Duck, one of the maids who didn't say much of anything to anyone.

I stood, looking around at the gleaming tables that where women wearing furs and men wearing finely cut suits would sit. I needed to get back to work.

"You've got a nice voice."

I whirled around. Marvin Whitman, the club's manager, stood right behind me. He was the one who took care of the day business at the Royale. His family owned the club, and it was his younger brother, Francis, who kept people coming to the club and charmed everyone from the musicians to the maids. Francis was tall and lean, with golden hair that flopped just so over his pecan-colored eyes. We all had a crush on him. He had a way of smiling that made it seem like God had given him those deep dimples just to make you happy. I'd seen him make a fifty-year-old grandmother blush like a teenager.

Marvin was nothing like his brother. He was short and squat, with bowed legs and a mean, crooked grin. He was almost completely bald except for several strands of greasy hair atop his pale scalp. The only thing he had in common with Francis was the color of their eyes. Except for a glint of malevolence, Marvin's eyes were flat.

"Thank you, Mr. Whitman."

He grinned at me and leaned close enough for me to smell the garlic on his breath.

"Call me Marv, darling."

Francis Whitman could make a woman swoon with one endearment. Marvin's "darling" was revolting. I looked down at my feet and clenched both hands around the broom handle.

"I should get back to work, sir. Sorry if my singing bothered you. It won't happen again."

"Now, how could the sound of an angel bother me?" His voice was low, raspy. "Don't rush off just yet. Surely, you have time to talk to your own boss?"

I looked up at him. This was the first time he had spoken to me, although I had heard many stories of his dealings with other maids at the club. He had made vaguely threatening advances to almost all the other girls, but no one said much about the details of those advances. We all needed the work. It was an unspoken rule that a black woman had to pay a certain price to hold down a job. For some, Marvin Whitman was that price.

But I was the plain girl, the quiet one, and I'd done a pretty good job of staying off his radar. I hated myself for indulging, even for a few moments, my silly fantasy of singing on stage. It hadn't gotten me anywhere except the center of Marvin's attention.

I wanted to run away from his leer, the lingering look that took in everything from the sneakers on my feet to the scarf on my head. I hoped that he found me not just plain but ugly. I had never embraced being Duck until that moment, when it seemed like being the ugly duckling was the only thing that could save me.

He was watching me, waiting to see if I was bold enough to reject him outright. He sat down at one of the tables and motioned for me to join him.

"Yes, sir," I mumbled, sitting as far from him as I could.

"Marv," he reminded me.

I swallowed back bile and nodded. I was determined not to say his name out loud, not to give in to this attempt at forced intimacy. I watched his hands while he lit a cigarette and propped it between his swollen lips. I kept my eyes on the cigarette while he kept his eyes on my face.

"What is it they call you again?"

"Duck."

This struck him as funny. The orange tip of the cigarette bobbed when he chuckled.

"Duck. So you want to sing." It was not a question, just an affirmation of what we both knew from my three-minute performance for an invisible audience.

"I sing at church, sir." It was a lie. Maybe if he thought I was a good Christian girl, he would leave me alone.

He frowned and waved a hand in the air. "Church," he spat. It was like a curse. "I'm saying, you want to *sing*. Like Billie Holiday, Lena Horne. *Sing*."

It was all I ever dreamed of, but I would never admit it to him. I sat there, mute and uneasy.

"Come on, girl. I saw you up there on the stage. I know a singer when I see one."

He paused until I finally met his gaze. I knew right then what was coming next. A lazy, almost sensual smile spread across his face.

"You know, Duck, I think you and I could be friends. Good friends. And then, after we get to know each other better, you could stand up on stage for real and share that pretty voice with the rest of the world."

I stood up and grabbed my broom.

"No!"

I blurted it out before I could stop myself, before I could consider the consequences.

He raised one shaggy eyebrow and took a long drag on his cigarette before stubbing it out on the tabletop.

"No?" He tilted his head as if he hadn't heard me correctly.

"No, thank you. Sir." I whispered, my voice shaking.

"No, huh?" He moved quickly for a fat man. Suddenly, he was standing, pressing his pelvis against my hip, my upper arm pinched between his fingers.

"I can have you if I want you, *Duck*. And I'm done asking nicely."

I froze. The only movements were tears streaming down my cheeks. His face was inches from mine, his lips parted, touching mine, softly for a moment, then crushing my lips against my teeth. I tried to scream, but it came out muffled and wet with Marvin's saliva. His hands began to roam roughly over my body.

"Marv."

The voice was deep and calm, with just a hint of warning. Marvin pushed me away and turned toward the door. I fell against the table, coughing and wiping my mouth over and over, wondering if I could ever get his taste and smell off me.

Francis Whitman, already dressed in his customary tuxedo, stood watching his older brother with narrowed eyes. Marvin ran his hand over his head and straightened the collar of his shirt.

"Frankie, you know how these nigger girls are. Always trying to get ahead by opening their legs."

He tried to sound tough, but his voice cracked. Francis's expression never changed. Marvin waited a beat, then realized his brother wasn't going to answer. He brushed past Francis and left the room. I took a deep breath and exhaled into a sigh. Francis looked at me, his brown eyes filled with sympathy and regret.

"Are you okay?"

I wasn't, but I nodded. He glanced at the doorway where his brother had gone, and his mouth tightened into an angry line.

"My brother won't bother you again."

He didn't say how he would make this happen, but I believed him.

"Thank you, Mr. Whitman."

He gave me a small, sad smile. I straightened my scarf and looked around the room. There was still work to be done. Francis nodded as if he read my mind. He watched me for a moment as I went to take down chairs stacked on a nearby table.

"You know, I heard you sing, Delia. You won't be cleaning floors forever."

He left then. After a long while, I went back to work.

During the summer when I first came to Chicago, I liked to walk around the different neighborhoods. I especially liked to walk downtown and near Lake Michigan, looking at the large estates and tall buildings. But then blacks started trying to move into white neighborhoods like Englewood and Cicero, and there were riots. White people were angry that blacks were violating the unspoken segregation agreements, and disillusioned blacks discovered that the supposedly "free" North wasn't really free at all.

I didn't blame them, but I didn't have time to fight with white people. I could barely afford my tiny room in a house on the South Side, and I was working so many hours that I was too tired to venture anywhere, except to work at the Royale and back home. I had a little transistor radio that I listened to every evening before bed. I liked to lay there flat on my back, stretching out my back, sore from stooping and reaching all day to make the Royale pretty again for its nightly patrons. The news stations carried reports of the riots, the new war in Korea and the atomic bomb. It all seemed so far away from my little world, and I'd left Greenville to try to find goodness, not more sadness. I liked to listen to the rhythm and blues station. It sounded a little like the jazz that I loved, but it had a deeper bass beat, a more rocking rhythm that made me feel as though I was listening to history being made. And there was something about Roy Brown, Louis Turner and Jimmy Witherspoon that lifted my sprits after a long day.

My room was small, but the house was a nice place, run by a widow who'd lived in the house her whole life. It was in the northern section of what people called the Black Belt, the older section where many of the homes were run down or converted into rooming houses for people like me: women with no family nearby, who worked long hours and kept quiet. The house showed its age, with its bricks faded to gray and just a tiny patch of lawn. But it was clean, and my room was bigger than the one I'd had back in Greenville. And unlike my childhood room, it was all mine. I'd used the little extra money I had, after paying for rent and food, to buy a white chenille bedspread, some inexpensive wooden bookcases, and my radio. I put a rag rug on the floor and I kept the room swept and neat. It wasn't much, but I took pride in the first place that was truly mine.

Some of the other women in the house were older. They had been married and had raised kids before leaving the South for Chicago's urban landscape. They kept photos on top of their dressers and beside their beds, testaments to lives beyond the rooming house and the Black Belt. At dinner, they exchanged stories across the kitchen table, sometimes realizing they were third cousins or they had both known "Junebug" back in Birmingham. I just listened and tried to smile, and I changed the subject whenever anyone asked me about my family.

I had no photos of my mother, of Merline, of Greenville. I had escaped to a city that was colder than I had ever imagined a place could be. I was twenty, and it was my third Chicago winter. It got cool in the winter in Greenville, but nothing like this bracing cold. I didn't even know the temperature could go below zero until I moved here, the wind making my face feel as if it might crack. I wore my coat collar up, a scarf hiding everything but my eyes, and still, I felt chilled to the bone every moment of the winter months. I spent winter nights huddled close to the radiator, trying to warm bones that seemed to freeze during the bus ride back to my room. And even though Chicago was cold, no one said hello on the street, and the Marvin Whitmans of the world believed they had the right to touch me, I didn't miss home a bit. When I thought of Greenville, I didn't remember the summers of my childhood. I didn't remember the singsong drawl that still marked me as a Southerner.

When I thought of Greenville, I remembered Rollins.

He was my mother's new husband. Everyone called him by his last name. When I was twelve years old, life wasn't perfect, but I felt safe with Mother. But when she met Rollins, everything changed.

I didn't have any physical reminders of my old life, but three years away had taught me that the memories were never too far away. It had been a long day, and I was tired. I turned my radio to the jazz station and set it right next to the head of my bed. I let Louis Armstrong erase my mind and lull me to sleep.

CHAPTER 8

"Come on Home"

Merline
Greenville, 1952–1953

The April 1952 edition of *Ebony* featured a quiz: "Which Is Negro? Which Is White?" Merline wasn't much of a reader, but the colored grocery store stocked the magazine and she couldn't resist picking it up and looking inside. It just didn't make sense. Negroes weren't white and whites weren't Negroes. She opened to the quiz and studied the photos. The women had wavy or straight hair, thin lips and skin that, in the black and white photos, looked nearly colorless. The men had slim, straight noses and wore expensive-looking ties and jackets. Merline frowned and looked around the store, as though she expected the editors to walk up to her and explain themselves. All of these people looked white. There weren't any colored people on the page as far as she could see.

She squinted at the small print at the bottom of the page and read the names of each person, none of which was familiar. She flipped to the next page for the quiz answers.

All the people pictured were Negroes, according to *Ebony*. She read the text of the article, which detailed the heritage and accomplishments of each person. Merline grew bored and flipped back to the photos. One woman looked familiar, and it took her several minutes to realize that the woman reminded her of Katherine. Certainly, her daughter was prettier than this woman, who had neither golden curls nor dark brown eyes like Katherine. But there was something familiar in the set of the woman's jaw, the look of determination in her eyes. This woman, according to the article, had often been mistaken for white.

Merline chuckled to herself. She had never known Katherine to be mistaken for white. But she stopped laughing when she considered that this might be because Katherine only went out with her light-skinned but clearly colored mother. She wondered if the woman ever let people think she was white. She could imagine it being easier to do so, the same way she had let people think she had been raped by a white man and Katherine was the result. This made her damaged goods, and thus unappealing to any eligible colored bachelors. But it was easier for her to let people feel sorry for her than to reveal the truth about her and Kenny.

But it was hard on Katherine, who went to the local colored school, the same elementary school that Merline had attended. She was the palest of all the children, and they made fun of her.

"Half-breed," they called her.

"High yellow."

"White bitch."

Nine-year-old Katherine had come home crying from school her first day of fourth grade. The girls had accused her of thinking she was better than everyone else. They said she "talked white," said her yellow hair looked stringy, called her fair skin pasty.

Merline had assumed Katherine's feelings were hurt and tried to comfort her.

"Kids sometimes say mean things to each other, Kat. Ignore them and they'll stop," she said, hugging her daughter close.

But Katherine pushed her mother away. "I wish I could go to the other school. I'm white, just like the girls who live across the street. Why can't I go to school with them?"

Merline swallowed the lump in her throat. "Katherine, you're not white. You're colored, like me."

Her face contorted into a grimace. "I'm not like you. I'm not!" she shouted, running to her room and slamming the door. Merline wanted to follow her, to try to explain how these things worked in Greenville, in the world. But she didn't know how to explain something that was just an accepted part of what she had known her entire life. This was just the way it was, but she knew that wouldn't satisfy Katherine. She turned to leave the room and saw Mrs. Banks standing there, watching her. Their eyes met for a long moment, and then Merline lowered hers, not wanting to seem impudent. But she wondered how much the woman had heard, and even after she excused herself to the kitchen to prepare for dinner, she couldn't stop thinking about the small smile on Nancy Banks's face.

It was that look she remembered as she put the *Ebony* magazine back on the rack and finished her shopping.

It wasn't until she was twenty-seven years old that Merline realize just how lonely her life had become. Katherine was nine and no longer a baby. She didn't need her mother for much anymore, and Merline found herself spending more and more time staring out of windows or in her small room, alone.

She didn't have any girlfriends, something that wasn't new but was suddenly unbearable. When Merline was a teenager, she was the kind of girl that boys liked and girls didn't—for the same reasons. But back then she had Kenny, and the business of keeping their secrets had taken up much of her time. And then there was Katherine to worry about, and there wasn't much time to think and wonder. But now, Merline's chores around the Banks home seemed to take up less time, and there was more time to contemplate all the ways in which her life seemed like nothing much to brag about.

Then there was the rest of the world, which seemed to be on the verge of some monumental shift. Greenville had been much the same for all her life, but things were changing. There had been so many lynchings when Merline was a small girl that colored people had resigned themselves to silence in order to avoid death.

But in 1952, there was a small but growing group of vocal citizens who held meetings and demanded to be called "Negro" instead of colored. Merline was never invited to any of these meetings, but she heard things when she shopped and on the rare occasions she went to church. Women gossiped about articles they had read in a new magazine called *Ebony*, and a black man had won the Nobel Peace Prize for doing some kind of work with the United Nations. She had learned this from watching the television news while the Banks family was on vacation one Christmas; she wasn't allowed to watch the television otherwise, because it was in the living room where the family entertained.

Of course, Katherine was allowed to watch whenever she wanted, and this was one of the developments that made her mother jittery. Her daughter knew more about the world outside Greenville than she did.

"Senator McCarthy is going to make sure the communists don't take over," Katherine told Merline.

"Senator who?"

This was at the beginning of Katherine's know-it-all phase, and Merline was not prepared for the look of disdain that passed over her daughter's pale face.

"Miss Nancy says we might get a color television soon," she told Merline the next year. By this time, she was afraid to reply to her daughter's pronouncements because feeling dumber than a nine-year-old made her want to cry. So she nodded and wondered at Katherine's use of "we," as if she were a true part of the Banks family and Merline was an outsider. Technically, this was true, and the Bankses certainly treated her like family, but she was certain Katherine didn't know just how truly a Banks she was.

In fact, Katherine had never even met Kenny, since he had not come home to Greenville during her lifetime. Merline knew better than to ask, but when Mr. Banks was feeling charitable, he passed along tidbits from Kenny's life. Boarding school was followed by college at Yale, although Mr. Banks would have preferred his son to attend a fine Southern university.

"But that just wasn't possible," he would say, glancing at Merline as if it was her fault that Kenny was spending his time in the North instead of in Texas where he belonged. "We Banks men have always attended college in Texas, and I told Kenny not to bring home any Yankee nonsense."

When he said this, Merline's spirits had soared because his words seemed to imply that Kenny would come home. But he never did, and after a while, she learned to stop hoping because it hurt too much. She just took each day as it came until she was twenty-seven and it seemed that everything was changing.

That summer, Merline bought a small radio to keep in her room, to try to keep up with Katherine. She learned that a novel by a black man, Ralph Ellison, was one of the most popular books in the country. She listened to the soap opera *The Guiding Light* until it switched to television. She learned that Rocky Marciano was the best boxer in the world, and she heard jazz bebop for the first time. Soon, she no longer had to pretend to know the random facts her daughter threw at her to prove she was smarter than her mother. But this was small victory, since the girl spent most of her free time either reading books that Merline couldn't understand or discussing those books with Nancy Banks.

But Merline found that listening to the radio kept her calm; if things were changing, she might at least know about those changes when they happened. The voices on the radio became her friends, and for a time, her loneliness abated.

Thanksgiving was colder than usual in 1953, the type of gray, windy day that chilled Merline to her bones and made her yearn for the near-100-degree days of a Texas August. She wore an old sweater that used to be her mother's all day, taking time to shiver in between cooking for the Banks's annual Thanksgiving party. They didn't have a large extended family—Mr. Banks was an only child, and his parents had died young. Each year, he told his wife that he had no intention of dining with her hillbilly relatives from Arkansas.

Each year, Merline roasted an immense turkey under the close supervision of Mrs. Banks. Katherine sat at the kitchen table, watching with the sullen look that had become her default facial expression.

"You could help peel the potatoes," Merline suggested, bending to baste the turkey.

"Oh, just let her rest. After all, she's been working hard at school," Nancy Banks said, taking a seat next to Katherine at the table. "We're very proud of you for getting all A's on your exams."

She beamed at Katherine, who smiled shyly. Merline turned her back and rolled her eyes. Those two were always grinning at each other while she did all the work. She resented Nancy's interference with Katherine, and although she tried to dismiss the feeling, she was hurt that her daughter seemed to prefer the white woman to her own mother.

"Did you baste the turkey yet? Last year it was a little dry."

Merline kept her back turned, giving a noncommittal "mmm-hmm" in response. Couldn't the woman see that she was basting the damned bird right now? But she wasn't allowed to talk back, to show anger, to stand up for herself. She had made a deal with the devil, she sometimes thought. In exchange for a place to live and work, she was to always be indebted to Nancy Banks. Taking a deep breath, she reminded herself that she had given up her own life so that Kenny's daughter would have a roof over her head. She glanced over at Katherine and Nancy, who flipped through a fashion magazine, giggling and exclaiming over dresses and hairstyles. Merline wiped her brow and remembered a time when she had been the kind of girl who cared about dresses and makeup.

"I'll start working on those potatoes," she announced, as if anyone cared. Nancy waved a hand at her and Katherine didn't even bother to look up.

Later, while Nancy and Kendall Banks entertained their guests in the dining room, Merline and Katherine ate their meal at the kitchen table. Katherine, dour and sullen, rebuffed her mother's attempts at conversation or muttered one-word replies that made Merline feel sad and irritated at the same time. She had resigned herself to eating in silence when Katherine spoke.

"Who is my father?"

Merline stopped chewing, the mashed potatoes turning to sour mash in her mouth. She swallowed with some difficulty. When Katherine was a small child, she had often asked about her family, in particular her father. In that relentless way of children, she had asked the question so many times and in so many ways that Merline had run out of evasions and half-truths. She had wanted to tell Katherine about Kenny, about how much in love they had been, about how much she resented his parents for sending him away to boarding school.

Of course, it was impossible to say any of this. So she had crafted a complete lie, something that had satiated Katherine until this moment.

"He was a soldier, Kevin Brown. He died in the war. I told you all of this, remember?" Merline tried to keep her voice from shaking.

Katherine frowned. "But I want to know more about him. I must look like him, right? Do you have a picture of him? Why isn't your last name Brown? Where is his family? Why don't we ever see them?"

Her daughter's stare was unwavering, as if she was searching Merline's face for the slightest hint of dishonesty. Merline kept her features neutral, giving nothing away.

"Why are you suddenly so interested in him? He's gone and it's just us. That's just the way it is."

Katherine slammed her fork down on the table. "Why won't you answer any of my questions?" She paused, waiting for a response. In the silence, they could hear the remote sound of laughter coming from the other side of the house.

"I'm going upstairs to read," Katherine announced, pushing her half-eaten dinner away.

"You should finish your food. You'll be hungry later." Instantly, she wished she could take the words back.

"Miss Nancy says a lady never cleans her plate. She said it's uncouth to eat so much," Katherine sneered, pointedly looking at Merline's empty plate.

Merline wasn't exactly sure what "uncouth" meant, but she got the idea. She stood and began clearing the table, crashing plates together loudly, not caring if they broke.

"You know what, Katherine? Miss Nancy is not your mother. I am. And no matter what you think of me, you will not speak to me that way." She stopped, glaring at her impudent, ungrateful, beautiful daughter. "Do you understand?"

Without another word, Katherine stalked out of the room. As she left, Merline thought she saw a look of shame flash in her daughter's eyes, but it came and went so quickly that she couldn't be sure.

Merline looked at her watch. It was time to serve dessert. She took off her sweater and put on the apron Mrs. Banks liked her to wear when company came over. She threw back her shoulders and pasted a professional smile on her face.

In the dining room, she took away the dinner dishes and brought back plates of pumpkin, lemon, and apple pies on a rolling serving cart. She stood still by the door, waiting for the signal to begin serving. Merline had been in this room hundreds, maybe thousands of times before, dusting the shelves of the glass-fronted china cabinet, polishing the surface of the rectangular table that seated twenty-four when fully extended. Before this holiday, she had spent hours polishing the silver to a high shine.

But she had seldom seen the formal dining room lit by long, tapered candles or heard the murmured conversation of moneyed guests. She had seldom smelled the potent mixture of expensive perfumes and Cuban cigars, or watched amber liquors being sipped from heavy crystal goblets that she would later hand-wash in the kitchen sink.

Nancy Banks sat at the far end of the table, and Kendall Banks held court at the near end. He wore his own custom-tailored tuxedo, and her gown was made of dark red satin that made her pale skin seem sallow in the dim light. She wore her golden hair waved softly away from her face and pulled up into a coil at the back of her head. Merline had often thought that Nancy Banks might have been pretty once, but now the pinched, suspicious look perpetually on her face made her unattractive. There was little doubt that life with Mr. Banks had made that expression a permanent feature of her face. He was casually dominant, leaving his wife to run the house, but interjecting and overruling whenever he saw fit. He made comments about her humble upbringing, making it clear to everyone in earshot that she had married up and he was nothing short of a saint for having saved her.

Mrs. Banks never protested or defended herself. She had always had household workers to do any manual labor, and now, she had her ten-year-old granddaughter to love. The only time the sour look left her face was when Katherine was in the room.

Seated between the Bankses were five couples, their bellies full of turkey and buttery side dishes that Merline had spent all day cooking. These were the people who controlled Greenville and other small towns like it around northeast Texas. Like Mr. Banks, many of them had made money in Dallas. Once their fortunes were secure, they had "retired" to smaller towns to control them like royalty in small kingdoms. They chose places like Greenville, invested their money in local causes, bought property and small businesses, and then slowly took over.

Merline watched them surreptitiously and thought to herself that as smart as Katherine was, there were still things about Greenville that Merline knew more about than her daughter did.

Mrs. Banks nodded, the signal for Merline to begin serving. She had just set down the final dessert plate when Kendall Banks cleared his throat and silenced the room.

"I have an announcement to make," he began, looking around the table into the eyes of each guest and smiling broadly. "As you know, it has been ten years since my only child, Kendall Junior, left for school back east."

Merline stood still and silent, looking down at the floor. No one ever mentioned Kenny in her presence. No one gave her updates about him or indicated in any way that he would be coming back home. Part of her had always hoped that he would, hoped that when he was a man and no longer a boy, he would come back for her. She wanted to take a deep breath, but didn't for fear of making a sound. It was pure luck that she was in the room at the moment of Mr. Banks's announcement, and she didn't want to ruin it by drawing attention to herself.

"Like any good Texas boy, my son has realized that there's no place like home. Kendall will be coming home to help me run the family business."

The guests clapped and began talking and eating, asking for details of Kenny's return and wondering whether he'd find Greenville changed after his experiences back East. Merline smiled. Kenny was coming home.

She looked up and found Kendall Banks staring into her eyes. He was no longer smiling, and his eyes held a warning that Merline had no trouble understanding. He held the gaze for a moment, and then his face changed. His features twitched and his mouth opened as if he wanted to cry out in pain. He made no sound. Merline winced at the brief look of agony that crossed his face just before his eyes went blank, as if a light inside his brain had been extinguished. His body fell back into his chair, then rolled over onto the floor.

Someone screamed. Someone else ran out of the room to find a telephone. The guests milled around the room, their voices a low rumble, asking if he would be okay, wondering why it took the ambulance so long, crying softly.

At first, Merline did not move. Then she began to move toward her room, followed by the sounds of Nancy Banks's sobs. Standing before the mirror, she felt as if she were looking at a stranger. She saw wavy black hair brushed back into a single braid that hung down her back. She saw skin the color of honey and cheekbones that gave her face an angular look. She saw a small waist, round hips, breasts that were fuller than they had been ten years ago. She slowly applied lipstick, watching the way her heart-shaped lips smoothed and shone under the color. She finally looked into her eyes and saw the fear there. She suddenly realized her entire body was shaking.

She was shocked by having watched a man die.

She was shocked because, at this moment, all she could think of was Kenny.

He was coming home.

CHAPTER 9
"Without A Song"

Violet
Greenville, 1927–1930

After Gray died, Violet discovered the power of words. Words could bring people together, as they had with her and Gray, but words were also useful for keeping people away. Violet developed her harpy's tongue carefully, trying out various ways to make sure that losing someone would never make her feel the way she had when Gray died.

It was difficult at first, because she still had Merline to care for, and the girl was too young to understand the dangers of love. Some days Violet shuddered when she looked at two-year-old Merline, with her cheerful smile and her long, wavy hair. Beauty was part of the problem with love. Beauty drew people toward you, made them persistent and foolish. She would have to be very clever to save this girl.

Violet herself had once been pretty, too. But Gray's death had dulled her eyes and left a permanent frown line between her eyebrows. She stopped caring about how she looked, and food became the only friend she would allow

SWAN

into her life. She did not cook except when absolutely necessary, and when she ate, she filled her stomach until it ached. She wore oversized, plain clothes that covered her thickening body, and she kept her hair in two tight braids on each side of her head. She wore no makeup or jewelry, and she stopped wearing the thin wedding band Gray had given her.

One of her neighbors ignored her better judgment and approached Violet one year after Gray's death. It was almost Christmas, a holiday that Violet had not acknowledged in any way. The house, as always, was spotless and orderly, but there was no Christmas tree, no stocking, no ornaments to suggest that this time of year was any different from any other.

Paulette Cross lived less than a mile away in a cabin much like the one Gray had built for his family. In fact, her husband, John, had worked labor jobs with Gray. John Cross was the one who had led Gray to these plots of land available to colored families. There were fewer than ten families living in the area in 1927, but the number would grow until there was an entire neighborhood of Negroes who did menial work for the whites of Greenville.

Paulette and Violet had been friendly before Gray died, but not exactly friends. The Crosses were in their early thirties and had four young children and, in 1927, had another on the way. They were busy working and parenting. Violet and Gray had only Merline, but lived in a cocoon of love that Paulette secretly envied. She saw them walking once when Violet was very pregnant, and they were so wrapped up in conversation with each other that they walked right by without seeing her.

Paulette had been one of the women who had helped Violet the day she learned of Gray's death, and she had cared for Merline during those early days when Violet was insane with grief and anger. Months had passed since then, and Violet had ignored or rebuffed Paulette's efforts at friendship with caustic language and narrow-eyed stares.

But it was Christmas, a time for camaraderie. Paulette attributed Violet's behavior to grief and went over to the Grimes's cabin carrying a large tray of homemade cookies and a large, red velvet stocking she had sewn for Merline.

Violet tried to ignore the knocking at her door. Merline was playing with a set of wooden blocks Gray had cut and sanded before she was born. Her mother sat at the kitchen table smoking a cigarette. She had recently begun smoking to give her hands something to do, to keep her mind focused on the rush of nicotine instead of what she had lost. It took a full year before she realized that thinking was part of the problem and if she kept busy, there would be little time for contemplation, crying, and rage. Emotions were a luxury that Violet was willing to leave to the rest of the world.

The knocking stopped and Violet thought that who-ever it was had gone away. But in a moment, the knocking returned and Violet heaved herself up from the table. She told a curious Merline to stay where she was and went to the door.

Paulette was determined not to leave without accom-plishing her mission, and no matter what Violet said

(Paulette disguised her shock at Violet's rude language) and no matter what Violet did (planting herself in the doorway with a wide-legged stance), she was going to get inside that house one way or another.

The two women went back and forth in the doorway for a long while before Merline's tinkling voice interrupted them.

"Cookie! Mama! Cookie!" She looked up at Violet, a pleading look in her eyes, her lower lip just slightly pushed out as if to show she was capable of a tantrum if pushed far enough.

Violet pursed her lips in what passed for a smile, rolled her eyes at Paulette and stepped aside.

After sending Merline off with a cookie in each hand, Paulette sat down at the kitchen table without waiting for an invitation. Violet sighed at the woman's persistence and reluctantly sat down in a wooden chair across the table from her. She found her matches in her pocket and lit a cigarette. Paulette, a member of the Second Baptist Church Women's Committee, did not approve of smoking, but she felt that a woman like Violet was entitled to a vice or two to get her through the days.

Paulette looked around the organized kitchen, with Merline's pile of blocks in one corner and the neatly ironed curtains at the window, pleased to see that Violet wasn't living in filth or neglecting her child, as was rumored. She knew better than to listen to gossip, especially from Second Baptist women who had been jealous of Violet's face and figure since the moment they'd met her. Now, she noted, that figure had grown plump, and the face had a hardness about it that had not been there before.

Violet smoked and waited. She had let Paulette in, but she reminded herself that even a friendship could be taken away, and she was not planning on dealing with any more loss. She would not allow the kindness in Paulette's dark eyes to beguile her. A tiny part of her yearned for someone to talk to, someone to laugh with, someone to fill the terrible quiet that filled her mind. But, no, it was too dangerous.

Paulette cleared her throat. "I've been worried about you. How are you, Violet?" Her voice was soft and sympathetic, but not pitying. She didn't feel sorry for Violet, unlike other people in town. She felt sorry that Violet had lost Gray, and, in her mind, there was an important difference between the two.

Violet noticed this distinction, her eyebrows raising slightly. Others had approached her with pity or condescending offers of help. They assumed they knew how she felt, knew what she needed. Paulette was the first person in a year to ask her how she felt.

Because she believed Paulette was sincere, she took her time answering.

"I am angry."

She was angry at the white men who had made an example of her husband. She was angry at her husband for insisting on what he called his "small moments of revolution." She was angry at herself for not listening to Rose, who had seen the truth about love. Angry.

Paulette nodded slowly. Others who had been rebuffed by Violet had said she was stuck-up and considered herself too good for their help. They had called her proud and difficult, and they had abandoned their efforts without trying to see things from her perspective. When they imagined how Violet must feel, they put her feet in their shoes instead of the other way around.

Paulette remembered how Gray and Violet had looked at each other. They had each other and needed no one else. She had felt jealousy when she first knew them, but now she felt a secret relief that she did not love John in a way that would make it impossible to love anyone else.

"What will you do?"

Violet finished her cigarette and stood up to pour two cups of coffee, not offering any sugar or milk when she shoved the second mug across the table to Paulette.

Merline had toddled back into the corner to play, her belly full of sugar and chocolate. She smiled sweetly at Paulette and Violet and then resumed unintelligible chattering as she stacked and knocked over the blocks.

The two women watched Merline for a moment. Violet's eyes were still on her daughter when she answered.

"I will take care of Merline. I'll make sure she eats, goes to school, has a place to live," she said, her voice low and cold. "But I can't love her. I loved Gray and I lost him."

Violet lit another cigarette, her eyes still on her daughter. Paulette looked from Violet to Merline, feeling overwhelmed by the tragedy that was unfolding before her eyes. She had never heard of such a thing, a mother who said outright that she would not love her child. She wanted to feel outrage, wanted to find words to shame Violet, to make her see that feeding and housing a child wasn't enough. Children needed love to grow properly.

But who was she to lecture this woman who had lost the most important person in her life? Paulette knew what it was to lose a loved one, and she would love her own children no matter what. Paulette absently rubbed her rounded belly, feeling for the kick of the six-month-old boy or girl growing inside her.

Violet finally looked back at Paulette, giving her that pinched hint of a smile. "I'll bet you're hoping for a girl," she said softly.

Paulette smiled. "After four boys, I think it's time I got a girl."

Violet nodded and stood, leaning over to snub her cigarette out in the ashtray. Taking her cue to leave, Paulette followed her over to the front door.

"If you need anything . . ." she began.

Violet shook her head. "You're a good person, Paulette Cross, and I thank you for coming over. But I can't be your friend. I hope you understand."

Paulette did, although that understanding made her want to cry. They bade each other goodbye, and walking home, Paulette said a prayer for Merline and Violet.

By 1930, Violet thought she had hardened her heart for good against any sweet-talking man brave enough to approach her. Not long after Gray died, Violet had discovered the deadening pleasures of alcohol, and she got so she could drink just enough to become numb, but not enough to get drunk. Prohibition made drinking a bit more trouble than it would later be, but people like Violet, people who needed to drink, found their ways to do so with minimal fuss.

She practiced drinking until she perfected the approach to that perfect peak, the point when her cheeks started to feel numb and her joints felt limber. She knew she had achieved that perfect buzz when her fellow drinkers seemed to think her smiles were genuine, when people spoke in a friendly manner but did not talk more than was necessary to maintain civility in the local drinking hole.

Bigger cities had speakeasies that catered to fancy crowds, but in Greenville, there were just a few small cabins that served as normal homes during the day, social clubs at night. These were run by entrepreneurial Negroes, usually young men with the energy, creativity and savvy to figure out ways to make the law look the other way. Violet's favorite spot was called Sonny's. It was not far from her house and she could walk over for a few drinks on Friday nights after Merline had fallen into a deep sleep.

Mostly couples and older single men patronized Sonny's. Violet was notable in that she was the rare young woman who drank at Sonny's but was not discreetly offering her services as well. A couple of men passing through Greenville had mistaken Violet for a working girl. The look in her eyes quickly disabused them of this notion. Sonny's regulars knew Violet and knew what she had lost, so they left her alone to her drinking. As long as Violet kept to herself and made no trouble for anyone else, people saw no reason to judge Violet's love affair with gin and juice.

Violet had begun to believe she was invulnerable to men, to love, to loss. But one night there was a new face at Sonny's. He was tall and lanky, a string bean of a man with sly eyes and a low laugh that sounded like velvet. Violet, as usual, spoke to no one as she nursed her drink, but she noticed that the newcomer came to Sonny's every Friday night for a month. On the fifth Friday, he approached her.

"You always drink alone?" His voice was deep and smooth, his words like a whisper in her ear, even though he had slid into the chair across from her at the small table for two that she always occupied alone.

It had been a long week for Violet. Merline was now five years old and asking about her father. She had told her daughter about Gray, but the child wanted to hear things over and over again, and every time Violet talked about Gray's life, she relived his death.

"I'm not looking for companionship. At least, not the kind that talks," she said, giving the stranger her most withering glare. It would have been enough to send a local man away, but Violet didn't know this man, who wore scuffed boots, a clean white shirt, and denim work pants. He had a closely trimmed goatee, which made Violet think he was vain.

Instead of leaving her table, he leaned back in his chair and grinned at her.

"You're tough, huh?"

She ignored him.

"Can I at least buy you a drink?"

Violet looked at her glass, She could feel the telltale numbness in her cheeks, her signal to finish the drink she had and head home to check on Merline and fall into a troubled sleep before waking the next morning with a headache and a furry tongue.

"Come on. One drink can't hurt, right?"

There was mischief in his smile, and Violet felt a flash of white pain in her belly, as it reminded her of Gray. She did not want to think of Gray, and now he filled her thoughts. Damn it.

She sighed. "Just one."

Violet woke up early the next morning, her head pounding, her mouth wooly. She turned her head on the pillow, and saw the stranger from Sonny's snoring next to her. She groaned softly with regret, remembering bits and pieces of the night before.

Nine months later, Duck was born. When her second daughter asked about her father, Violet refused to provide details, only saying there wasn't much to tell. It was true, in a way. She hadn't asked that stranger's name, and he hadn't asked hers.

CHAPTER 10
"Kiss of Fire"

Duck
Chicago, 1952

Every time I found myself mopping up after Marvin Whitman, I swore it would be the last time. Then, a month, a week, a few days later, I would find myself back in the same position, swabbing the mop back and forth to get rid of the evidence of another of his alcoholic binges.

He was always a drinker, but things had gotten worse lately. His brother Francis didn't want him around the club when he was drunk. It was expected, of course, that there would be drinking in the club, but Marv took things too far, stumbling through the door during the main acts, yelling out obscenities when the bartenders tried to corral him into the back room. I didn't see any of this for myself, since I cleaned during the days and was long gone by the time Marv made his appearances. I only saw the aftermath, his vomit on the floor, sometimes Marv himself passed out nearby. Francis was the one who told me how Marv had been acting the first morning I found Marv passed out on the stage. I was tempted to wake him with a jab of the broom handle, but I called his brother instead.

"Marv has these demons. He always has," Francis explained after he threw his brother into the back of a taxi.

I thought about Mother and Rollins, about Merline and all the secrets I had known.

"It seems to me that lots of people have demons." I wasn't willing to feel sorry for someone like Marvin.

Francis nodded. "Yes. But Marv never learned to deal with his the way most of us do."

I shrugged and poured soap into the mop bucket. When I looked back at Francis, he was watching me. I tried, and failed, to read the expression in his eyes.

"You think I'm making excuses for him."

His voice was flat, and I worried that I had crossed a line even though I hadn't said much. Francis was friendly to the crew, and he even joked with some of the men and offered them cigarettes when they ran low. But none of the other women who cleaned Club Royale ever spoke to Francis Whitman the way I did. I suspected they thought I was getting some kind of special treatment, but none of them knew that Francis had saved me from his brother. We never spoke of it afterward, but the incident created a certain intimacy between us, and I always thought of him as Francis, though I never called him anything except Mr. Whitman or sir. When we were alone, we talked, mostly about music or singers coming to the club. But when Marv's drinking got out of control, I was the one Francis asked to clean up. He didn't even have to ask me not to tell anyone. Somehow, he just knew I wouldn't.

"He's your brother. You're supposed to take care of each other." For a moment, I thought of Merline.

He shook his head. "But maybe I'm making it worse by propping him up. Cleaning up his messes."

We both looked down at the remnants of Marv's night.

"But what else could you do?"

He looked off toward the empty bar and I took the chance to take him in. He was dressed more casually than usual, his white Oxford shirt unbuttoned at the neck, khaki pants that looked like they had been tailored to fit him perfectly. His blonde hair flopped messily over his brow, and even with frown lines creasing his forehead, he was boyish and charming.

He turned back to me and I looked down quickly, hoping he had not caught me looking.

"I could fire him."

Everyone knew Marv didn't do any actual work, but that wasn't what Francis meant. Firing his brother would mean cutting off his allowance, refusing to let him in the club, forcing him to find his own way. Marv must have been forty years old. Too late to start over.

"You can't fire your own brother."

Francis sighed and stood up straighter, brushing his hands over his clothes.

"And I can't go on like this." He looked down at Marv's mess one more time, then left.

By Christmastime, I had cleaned up after Marvin Whitman many more times. I was friendly with a woman my age, Theresa, who also worked at the club, and she said there were rumors that Marv's brother was planning to fire him.

"You can't fire your own brother," I said, echoing the words I had told Francis three months ago.

Theresa sat lounging on a chair, watching me. I liked Theresa, but she was lazy. Technically, since I was now the crew chief, it was my job to tell Theresa to get back to work. But I liked her company. I think she liked me because I was the only one who didn't flinch at the sight of her. Her right cheek was scarred, the raised flesh glowing pink in contrast to the rest of her brown face. She came to Chicago to escape her old boyfriend, who had burned her face on a stove burner after she talked back to him.

"Francis Whitman can do anything he wants to do, fine as he is."

Theresa was so petite that her feet didn't quite reach the floor when she sat in one of the chairs. She liked to cross her legs and sit child-style instead. Her uniform skirt was too big for her, and it billowed out like a blanket over her crossed legs.

I liked Theresa because she said things that made me laugh, even when I didn't want to.

"You have a crush on Mr. Whitman?" I teased her.

Theresa wiggled her perfectly plucked eyebrows at me, making me smile.

"I would, but he only has eyes for you, Duck."

I stopped mopping. "Now you're just being crazy."

"I'm not crazy. I know what I know. And what I know is, Mister Francis gets a look in his eye when Miss Duck comes into the room."

No one had ever had a crush on me, as far as I knew, and I liked the strange idea of it. As much as I liked her, Theresa was a terrible gossip. She made no secret of this, so all the workers knew not to tell her anything they didn't want the world to know. So I wouldn't tell her how he talked to me like a friend when no one else was around. I wouldn't tell her that he had saved me from his brother two years ago. I wouldn't tell her that I sometimes dreamed of his hands touching my face as we kissed.

I pretended to dismiss the thought of Francis Whitman, changing the subject to other club gossip.

"And clean while you talk, please. I can't do everything myself."

Theresa gave me a salute, took the mop from me and started talking in her high, girlish voice. I let the sound of her chatter drift over me as I wiped the glass tabletops with a rag and wondered about Francis Whitman.

I was twenty-two years old, and for the first time in my life, I felt like a woman instead of a girl. Sometimes, when I looked in the mirror, I saw more than the plain little Duck I had been all my life. I had stopped wearing my hair in braids after Rose had dragged me to a beauty shop, where the stylist told me I had "good hair" and all it needed was a little pressing. Theresa was diligent about having her hair straightened and styled, spending what seemed like far too much of her money on vanity. I told her this once and she just laughed and told me that she had to make the best of what she had to find a husband, especially with a face like hers.

Pressing sounded as if it might be painful and I had no idea what it involved, not having listened to Mother and Merline when they talked about such things. But Theresa made me promise to sit still, so I sat back and closed my eyes. When I opened them, I saw a stranger in the mirror. My hair lay in soft waves, framing my face. I brushed my fingers over the back, stunned at how different it felt.

"You look beautiful!" Theresa said, appearing in front of me, her hair still in large green curlers.

I waved a hand at her. "Please. I've never been beautiful. But it does look nice, doesn't it?" I conceded.

Theresa put her hands on her hips. "You might not have been beautiful back in Texas, but you're beautiful now," she declared, returning to the hair dryer.

I looked up at the woman who had styled my hair, who was waiting for my reaction. I turned back to the mirror, and for the first time in my life, I liked what I saw.

The next day was Christmas Eve. The club would be open, so we were needed for cleaning during the day, but no one would work on Christmas. I arrived at work early, even the bitter cold wind not preventing me from preening at my reflection in the windows I passed. I wanted to get to work to go over the schedules for the next week, and this filled me with a sense of purpose and responsibility. I still didn't make much money, and I still longed to be on stage instead of cleaning floors. But I had a friend, Theresa, and Chicago had begun to feel like home.

Before I even turned on the light in the back room we used as a makeshift office, I knew something was wrong. It smelled as if someone had spilled a bottle of strong rum mixed with milk that had gone bad. In the fluorescent light, I saw Marvin Whitman slumped down in the corner. The lights and noise I made woke him. He blinked several times before my presence registered in his mind.

I stood still. I had not been alone in a room with Marvin Whitman since the day he pressed his lips against mine as I struggled. I remembered the slimy feel of his mouth on my face, the acrid smell of his sweaty drunkenness. Frozen, it took me a few moments to realize that Marvin was no longer slouched on the ground. He was on his feet and lurching closer to me. I opened my mouth to scream, and the sound that came out was more animal than human. There was no one else in the building, and Marvin grew steadier on his feet with each step.

The next minutes happened in fragments as I drifted from horror to sadness to resignation. He pushed me to the floor. The feel of his belt buckle pressing into my abdomen. His frenzied whispers in my ear, uttering filth and madness. His porcine grunts. Unimaginable pain. Then punching, hitting, slapping. I felt my lips swelling, vision blurring, teeth cracking. The taste of blood in my mouth, streaming down my face, pooling into the well between my chin and chest. Kicking, kicking until breathing hurts so much I want to stop, stop breathing forever, anything to make it end. But it never ends, it goes on and on until my whole body feels like it's on fire.

When it was finally over, I lay on my back, staring at the ceiling. I listened to the sounds of Marvin zipping, buttoning, threatening me with worse if I told. I listened long after he stumbled out of the room, long after the front door, the club slammed shut. When I closed my eyes, there was just silence.

I looked around the room. The walls were pale green, and, when I turned my head to one side, I could see the gray sky through a rectangular window. I tried to lift my head, and a searing pain seized me. I cried out. My voice sounded funny. I closed my eyes and pushed my tongue around the inside of my mouth. My top front teeth were gone. Images flashed through my mind, remembering. I became aware of a beeping sound that I hadn't noticed before. I opened my eyes again and turned, slowly, to look at the other side of the room. There was a chair and it took me a while to focus on the person sitting in it. Francis Whitman.

My mind felt fuzzy, as if my brain was covered with cotton. But the fuzz was just temporary, and in a few minutes, clarity arrived and I found that I missed the short-lived cotton that hid the truth. I remembered it all.

My eyes met his. Tears streamed down his cheeks when he looked into my eyes, and I began to cry, too. Francis came to the side of the bed. He opened his mouth but nothing came out. He seemed to be trying out different words in his mind before he finally spoke.

"Can I call your family for you? You shouldn't be here without your family."

I shook my head, wincing. "No family." My voice was weak, ragged.

He nodded and looked down at his shoes. "I suppose we have that in common, now."

I shuddered. "What about—" I stopped, unable to say the name.

He shook his head and took a deep breath. Wiped his tears away with the back of his hand, a childlike gesture.

"He used to be different, you know. I know you probably don't care. But it's important to me that you know that he used to be different."

I didn't want to hear anything about Marvin, and it must have shown on my face. But Francis was looking out the window as he spoke.

"We both went to the best schools in Chicago. He was only one year older than me, so we were always together. He went away to college first, Columbia. He was going to study business. I got into Julliard. But when I got to New York, he was already different. We had always been best friends, but suddenly, he changed. He was wild in those days, drinking, dope. He ended up dropping out of school. Later, when I came back to Chicago, he followed me, promising to get clean. And he was okay for a while, helping me with the club."

He stopped abruptly. I was acutely aware of the damage Marvin had done, to my body, to my soul. A small part of me acknowledged that Francis, too, was hurt, but in a different way.

"What did you play? At Julliard."

"Piano," he whispered.

I looked at his hands, the long fingers, the soft skin. When he started to speak, his voice was still a whisper.

"We argued. After they found you, they called me. I knew it was him. Because of the other time. I just knew." He stopped and his shoulders slumped. "And he stormed out of the club, into his car. An hour later, I got a call. They brought him here."

He must have seen something in my eyes, panic that showed that I didn't understand.

"No, no. He can't hurt you anymore. There was an accident, he drove into a tree. He's dead."

Now he perched on the side of my bed and sobbed. "I am so sorry, Delia," he mumbled through his tears. "Sorry, so sorry."

I shouldn't have felt anything except relief that Marvin was gone, that he could never touch me again. The relief was there, but the strongest feeling I had was sadness. I felt sad for me, sad for Francis. I watched him cry, wondering whether he was crying for me, for Marvin, or for some other reason that was too complicated to name.

I waited for him to calm before I spoke the first words that came to mind.

"What day is it?" I croaked, hating the sound of the words lisping through the space where my teeth used to be.

He wiped his face with his handkerchief and handed me a fresh one from his jacket pocket.

"It's Christmas Day." He paused and looked out the window as if he was thinking about what to say next. "How do you feel?"

I raised my head and ignored the stabbing pain long enough to see the cast on my arm. My other hand went to my face, touching the contours of the lumpy mess Marvin's evil had left behind. I realized I could only see through one eye, but I could see that Francis wanted me to be okay, that he wanted me to tell him that I would survive. But I couldn't stop the tears from coming, even though I wanted to be strong, I wanted to be okay.

I opened my mouth to lie, to say that I was fine, to smile for him. Instead, he leaned over and brushed his fingers over my forehead.

"Don't talk, Delia. I can see how you feel."

He called for a nurse and they came quickly, bringing a clear liquid that went into the IV bag, through a tube, and into my arm. Soon I dozed, watching Francis sit back in his corner chair, thinking about the feel of his fingers on my skin. Soft, gentle, protective.

He spoke softly just before I slept.

"I'll make this up to you, Delia. I will take care of you."

I was in the hospital four more days before I was released. I dreaded the bill that I would receive, knowing that I couldn't pay.

"Don't worry, Miss Dukes. Your bill has been paid," the nurse told me when I asked.

"Who paid it?" I asked, though I knew.

She flipped through papers attached to a clipboard.

"Mr. Francis D. Whitman. He said your injuries were work-related and that he, as your employer, was responsible."

She pulled an envelope from between two sheets of paper and handed it to me. It contained a card with a dentist's address and phone number, and a note from Francis.

"There is a driver waiting for you outside. He'll take you to the dentist," it read in his flowery, almost feminine script.

The nurse leaned over, trying to read the words, but I held the paper tilted enough to hide the words.

"You're lucky, you know, to have such a generous employer," she told me, giving me a professional smile. "Soon enough you'll be as good as new."

I didn't feel at all lucky. I pressed my lips together and tried to smile while hiding the space where my front teeth had been. She could only see the outside and she didn't see that inside I was different, that I would never be the same. My bruises were fading and my arm would heal. I was grateful that Francis was helping me, but I couldn't imagine ever feeling like myself again. It was as if Marvin took the real me with him to the grave, and I was left with this new self, a timid, emotional woman who was constantly on the verge of tears and who no longer knew how to smile properly.

Francis had insisted I take as much time off as I needed, and I did, visiting the dentist several times to be fitted for false teeth, learning to cook with one hand, watching my face return to normal. I spent my days listening to the radio and thinking about what to do next. I doubted I could continue to work at the club, not with everyone watching and whispering about what Marvin had done to me. I didn't even talk to Theresa when she called or sent notes to my house. Our innocent, easy friendship was no longer possible. I was damaged goods.

By the end of January, I had found several cleaning jobs that might be right for me. None of them was in a nightclub, or even in the same part of the city as the Club Royale.

On the last Friday in January, I went down to the Royale to retrieve a few personal things from my locker. I still had my door key, and I let myself in early that morning. It was a crisp winter day, cold and sunny, and I left my coat on inside the club because the heat was not turned on.

I walked quickly through the main room, avoiding the back room where Marvin had raped me. I felt bile rising in my throat as I passed by the door, but I took a deep breath and kept moving. This had been my strategy during the past month. The less I allowed Marvin to contaminate my thoughts, the more I was able to get through each day. It had reached the point where he only came in my dreams, which I could not control. I tried thinking of Francis Whitman at night, trying to control my dreams through sheer will, but it was Marvin Whitman's nasty smile that awakened me in the middle of the night.

That was why I had to leave the Royale for good. I thought that leaving Francis behind would allow me to leave Marvin behind for good, too.

The maids' locker room had a faintly musty smell, as if Theresa and the others had been neglecting the far corners where dust could hide. When I was the crew chief, before everything changed, the room had always smelled fresh. Theresa used to tease that I cleaned more than I needed to just to impress Francis Whitman.

When I opened my locker, I noticed a small square envelope lying on top of my neatly folded uniform. Inside was a sheaf of crisp bills and a card.

The card was an invitation, announcing the debut performance of the Club Royale's newest singer, Delia Dukes. The date was three weeks ahead, on a Thursday night. In Francis's handwriting were instructions for me to use the money to buy a dress and shoes for my big night.

My heart beat faster and I looked around the room, as if the walls could explain things to me.

I went out to the main ballroom, took a chair down off the table and sat, thinking about the day I stood on stage, broom in hand, singing "At Last."

Now I would have the chance to sing for real.

But then came the questions: Was it a bribe? Should I say no, tell Francis that I couldn't be bought? Or was it a peace offering, a way to make up for what his brother had done?

Part of me wanted to feel insulted. Did he think that this could make up for what I could never get back? But part of me, the bigger part, couldn't resist the idea of this one-in-a-million chance to sing, to try to see if I could be more than just a maid from Greenville, Texas.

I stared at the stage, weighing my choices. I could choose my pride, or I could choose my dream.

On Thursday, February 14, 1952, I performed on stage for the first time.

CHAPTER 11

"Secret Love"

Merline
Greenville, 1953–1955

Kendall Banks was gone and the Banks home felt empty without the smell of his cigar smoke and the echo of his booming voice ringing through in the halls. Merline had assumed an elaborate funeral would be held soon after Kendall Banks's death, but she overheard Nancy on the telephone saying that there would be a private family funeral and a formal memorial service later, when Kenny could be present. Her son, who was currently traveling in Europe, needed time to wrap up his affairs, she told the caller, so honoring her husband would have to wait.

Kenny would not be home until just before Christmas. Nancy Banks alternated between organizing the biggest funeral Greenville had ever seen and making sure everything in the house reflected the season appropriately. There were decorations to hang and preparations to be made for Kenny's arrival.

"We can't just cancel Christmas," Nancy snapped when Merline seemed to question the propriety of putting up the lights just days after her husband's death on Thanksgiving. "It's Kenny's favorite time of the year."

Then Mrs. Banks rushed from the room, sobbing, leaving a relieved Merline alone to her thoughts. And all she could think of was Kenny.

What would he look like now after all these years? Would he still smell like citrus? Would she now seem boring in comparison to the women he'd met in college and while traveling? After all, she had gone nowhere and done nothing in his absence. Well, not exactly nothing, she thought, glancing at Katherine. Her daughter sat on the sofa in the sitting room, her head stuck in a book instead of helping Merline with the decorations.

"It wouldn't kill you to help me," Merline snapped. She was annoyed by the way Katherine kept reading, looking up only after she had finished the sentence she was reading.

"Katherine should focus on her studies, don't you think, Merline?" Nancy Banks said from the doorway.

She was always skulking around, spying and interfering. Some days, Merline suspected that Nancy wanted to get rid of her altogether and have her granddaughter all to herself.

"You don't want the girl to end up in a dead-end job with no prospects, do you?"

Like her mother. Merline sighed and went back to work untangling strings of tiny white lights, willing herself not to say something she would regret. Nancy Banks never tired of reminding her that she had saved them. In exchange, she was expected to take whatever Mrs. Banks dished out. Most of the time, she accepted this as the price she must pay for giving her daughter a home, and even when Katherine was rude, Merline focused on the positive: Katherine was bright, capable, and attractive. She would go far in life, Merline was sure of this, and if it meant sacrificing her own dignity to Nancy Banks' derision, well, it was worth it.

Her own mother had kicked her out of the house, had not once come to see her or Katherine. In quiet moments, she mourned the loss of the feeling that, no matter what, her mother would always be there. It wasn't Mother she missed so much as the sense of being connected to family.

It was her job to give that feeling to Katherine, and she was trying to do this the best way she knew how. Katherine had what Merline did not, and it was because of Nancy Banks. So she was not in a position to protest that her daughter was slowly, but surely, being taken from her.

Kenny arrived the week before Christmas. The house had never looked more inviting. A six-foot Douglas fir filled one corner of the formal living room. It was strung with white lights and featured glass ornaments Nancy Banks had collected over the years. Each window on the first floor featured real pine wreaths, each with a single red velvet bow at the top center. Merline had been ordered to keep a simmering pot of cinnamon, cloves, and other spices on the stove at all times.

Nancy had taken Katherine shopping in Dallas, and Merline had to admit her ten-year-old daughter had never looked prettier. She wore a full pink and white polka-dotted skirt with a white poodle pictured on it. Her white shirt had cap sleeves and a rounder collar, and she had tied a pink silk scarf around her neck. Her hair was tied up, with the ponytail spiraling down her back. There was a hint of matching lipstick on her mouth, and she wore black ballet flats with tiny pink bows.

The look had been copied from one of the magazines Nancy and Katherine loved. Nancy wore one of her best dresses as well, and Merline felt underdressed in the drab black uniform that she wore at Mrs. Banks's insistence. She suspected the woman wanted her to look as unattractive as possible, and as they all waited in the sitting room, she smoothed her hair back, sat up straight, and hoped Kenny would see her as he had when they were teenagers.

Merline wondered what Nancy had told Katherine about Kenny. She had been so focused on her own excitement that, until that moment, she had not considered Katherine's reaction to her father. Of course, she didn't know Kenny was her father, but she was a smart girl—how long would it take her to see the resemblance between herself and Kenny? Merline looked at her daughter, who had Kenny's pale skin, his light hair, and most strikingly, his smile. It was her smile, which lately she saw little of, that reminded her so much of Kenny. She looked at Nancy, who sat chattering nervously to Katherine. Had she told the girl that she was, in fact, her grandmother? Could that be why Thanksgiving was the last time she'd asked about her father?

Merline was startled when the doorbell rang. She took a deep breath and followed Nancy and Katherine to the door.

Standing a step behind her daughter, she couldn't help being surprised at how much Kenny had changed. His unruly white-blond hair was cropped short in the back and the front was slightly longer, parted on the left and combed neatly to the side. He was taller, which seemed improbable since he was almost grown when he left for college. Maybe it was the crisp white shirt he wore with a dark suit that had clearly been tailored to fit. Maybe it was the emerald tie that reflected the precise color of his eyes and made his suit seem less somber. His skin was still pale and smooth, but now a neat mustache framed his lips.

He went by Kendall now, something she had overheard Nancy telling a friend. This man standing in the hallway, hugging his mother and answering her barrage of questions, was Kendall. She didn't know him.

Then he smiled, and in his crooked grin Merline saw the boy he'd been. Kenny.

Slowly, she emerged from her reverie to listen to what Nancy was saying. She was introducing Kenny to Katherine, who shook his hand politely and curtsied just as Nancy had taught her to do. She blushed when Kenny laughed, proud of herself. Merline winced at the sound of her daughter's proud laughter. She knew the danger of thinking being pretty was enough in life. She knew how much Katherine liked being the center of attention. She had been the same way when she was younger. The last ten years had taught Merline the perils of pride. She wished she could tell Katherine what she'd learned, but Merline suspected it was the kind of lesson that can only be learned the hard way.

"Katherine is Merline's daughter," Nancy said, her voice formal and stiff.

They all stood there for a moment, secrets hanging between them. Merline wanted to blurt out that Katherine was *Kenny's* daughter. She noticed an odd look on Katherine's face, wondering whether the girl might be the one to say something. She glanced at Kenny, searching his face for a spark of the fire that had made him believe in Merline and their baby all those years ago. He met her gaze, but she could see only sadness behind his smile.

"She is lovely," Kenny said simply, still looking at Merline.

Turning to Nancy, he cleared his throat.

"I have someone I want you to meet, Mother."

Just then, a woman appeared in the doorway behind Kenny.

"I'm so sorry, Mrs. Banks. I had to fetch my purse from the car, and Kendall simply could not wait to get home." She extended a smooth, manicured hand to Nancy.

"I'm Priscilla."

Kenny wrapped an arm around her waist. "Mother, Priscilla is my wife."

Priscilla spoke in a surprisingly husky voice that softened her clipped Yankee accent. She wore a sable jacket with a matching hat that Merline thought were much too heavy for Texas, even in December.

Nancy stood still for just an instant, then drew Priscilla into her arms, insisting that family did not stand on ceremony. She ushered Kenny and Priscilla into the sitting room and instructed Katherine to go along and play. She glanced at Merline, who remained in the entry hallway, her mouth hanging open.

Nancy looked as if she wanted to say something, but she didn't. Instead, a huge smile spread across her face. It was a grin of victory. Kenny was back, but Merline was firmly a part of his past, the smile said. It crushed Merline.

"Merline, do bring in a tray of refreshments. I'm sure Kenny and Priscilla are hungry after all that traveling." Nancy used her haughtiest tone, the smile still distorting her features.

Merline managed to hold in her tears until she reached the kitchen, where she took five minutes to let the salty drops fall from her eyes. Then she went back to work.

Priscilla Banks was small, no more than five feet tall, no more than 100 pounds. Somehow, she managed to be thin and curvaceous at the same time, and Merline, who was tall and had curves bordering on plumpness, felt like a lumbering giant next to the newest addition to the household. Her steps thumped while Priscilla's glided. Her hands were rough and calloused, while Priscilla's were soft and bejeweled. During the day, Merline tied her hair back in a bun and wore a scarf on top. Priscilla's hair was a thick mane of chestnut that she wore in a shoulder-length bob that waved charmingly around her face. Her eyes were the color of ripe limes, and her cheeks were rosy and full.

Merline spent the first day of Kenny's return keeping busier than usual and taking every opportunity to observe Priscilla. She listened as the woman described how she'd met Kenny at a Manhattan party. She had been studying literature at Sarah Lawrence. When she met Kenny, she knew that she had found her husband. She talked about her parents, her father a judge in Connecticut, her mother active in what Priscilla called "philanthropy." Merline did not know the word, but she assumed it was something rich people did to stay busy. Without explicitly saying so, Priscilla indicated she was rich, using codes and shorthand that even Merline understood. Judging by Nancy's deference to the woman, Merline guessed that Priscilla's family was much wealthier than the Banks family. Nancy clearly wanted to impress her new daughter-in-law, and Merline smiled grimly at the idea that Nancy Banks had been knocked down a few notches.

By nightfall, Merline was exhausted. She shuffled into the room she shared with Katherine, anxious to let sleep blot out the recriminations that kept running through her head. How could she have not imagined that

Kenny's life would have moved forward, even while her own was stuck in one place? How could she have entertained even the tiniest hope that Kenny would come home and rescue her, that he would meet his daughter and immediately insist that they be a family? She should have known that the idealistic boy she had loved would grow into someone she didn't recognize.

She hated Nancy for gloating. She hated Kenny for growing up, for not coming back to get her when his family sent him away. She hated Priscilla, who could have chosen anyone else from her social circle back East. She hated the weak part of herself that still believed in fairy tales, no matter how much evidence to the contrary life provided.

Katherine was lying on her bed reading. She didn't look up when her mother entered the room, and, for once, Merline didn't care. She undressed and got into her own bed, closing her eyes against the light of the reading lamp.

Merline's mind continued to race as she lay in her bed. After a while, she heard the rustling of Katherine's book and then the click of the lamp switch.

"Priscilla said I can wear her fur jacket sometime when I'm older," Katherine said into the darkness. "She was a model in New York during summers off school. Miss Nancy and I are sure we've seen her in a catalog. She said she's going to show me how to put on makeup, too. Miss Nancy said I'm too young, but Priscilla winked at me. She doesn't think it's ever too soon for a young lady to learn to make the most of her appearance."

Part of her liked the cheer she heard in her daughter's voice, but another part, the more cynical, worried part, thought that Priscilla and Nancy were determined to take everything from her, even her daughter. Katherine already adored her grandmother, and now she had yet another white woman to admire more than her own mother.

"Don't grow up too fast, Katie," was all Merline could think to say. She felt the tears from earlier in the day coming back to wet her cheeks, and she was glad the room was too dark for Katherine to see her crying. She hated this part of herself, the part that cried instead of fighting. But the past ten years had changed her both inside and out. Her mother and Duck wouldn't recognize Merline today, someone who simply let life happen instead of taking action.

But what action could she take? Certainly, she was not a prisoner in the Banks home. But what kind of life would Katherine have, living on the money her mother could earn elsewhere? Nancy Banks provided room and board and a small salary that was comparable to what other housekeepers earned, and Merline had some money saved. Her savings would get them started on a new life. But what would happen when it ran out? A maid's salary wouldn't even cover rent if she took her daughter and moved away. Like her own mother, she would have to work two jobs. And then who would look after Katherine? Nancy was no prize, but she did love her granddaughter.

"You don't want me to be happy, do you? You just want me to be like you, miserable and alone," Katherine whispered. Her voice was low but loaded with venom. "I would never settle for a life like this. I'll never be like you."

Merline didn't speak. She didn't move, not even to wipe away her tears. She listened as Katherine wrestled with her blanket until she found a comfortable spot. Soon, Katherine's breath grew deep and regular. Eventually, Merline's tears dried and left salty residue on her face. Eventually, her thoughts settled into a lump of regret, and still she lay there until dawn lightened the sky from black to gray and it was time to get up and face another day.

As Christmas Day approached, Merline avoided being alone with Kenny. She worked and focused on watching Priscilla, but she soon realized that Priscilla was watching her, too. On Christmas Eve, Kenny went out to do some last-minute shopping, and Nancy took Katherine to see a matinee showing of *The Nutcracker* in Dallas.

It was two o'clock in the afternoon, the time when Merline folded and ironed. She liked the afternoons, which were usually quiet. Today, she turned on the radio and was singing along with "I Saw Mommy Kissing Santa Claus" while she ironed. She never let other people hear her sing, because she was and had always been tone deaf, so she was embarrassed when she saw Priscilla standing at the entrance to the laundry room, her arms folded as she leaned against the doorjamb.

She clamped her lips shut and turned off the radio. She wondered how long Priscilla had been standing there, watching her with those piercing green eyes.

"I'm sorry if I disturbed you," Merline said politely, keeping her eyes on the dress she was ironing. It was one of Katherine's, an expensive blue cotton shift that Nancy had picked out for her granddaughter.

"We haven't had a chance to talk since I've been here, have we?"

Priscilla's tone was friendly, but when Merline looked up at her, she was not smiling. Merline didn't answer, since they both knew that, indeed, they had never had a real conversation, and Merline was content to keep it that way. She was already quite aware that she could not compete with Priscilla, and she got through the day by not allowing herself to think too much about Kenny.

"I know who you are." The friendliness in Priscilla's voice was gone, replaced by a warning, ominous tone.

"I am Merline Dukes. I work for the Banks family."

Priscilla narrowed her eyes. "Yes. And you, Merline Dukes, are the reason Ken's parents sent him away to school. You and your little bastard, that is."

Merline felt like throwing the iron at Pricilla, wanted to watch as the flat side marred Priscilla's perfect skin forever. Instead, she finished pressing the dress, set the iron down carefully and put the dress on a hanger. She could feel Priscilla's eyes following her every move, waiting for a response. Merline realized nothing she could say would make Priscilla go away, so she said nothing at all.

The silence angered the woman.

"If you think you have a chance to trap Kenny again, you can forget it. He told me all about how you seduced him, how you tried to use that baby as a way to hold on to him."

She paused and smiled. "But believe me, I am all that Ken wants now. He doesn't want you, and he doesn't want that little half-breed of yours, either."

Merline took a deep breath to keep herself steady. Kenny wouldn't say those things, would he? They'd been in love. She knew that. He'd loved her and he'd wanted to be with her and Katherine. No matter how much Kenny had changed over the past ten years, it didn't change the fact that they had once, in another lifetime, loved each other. Right?

She kept her expression blank to hide the doubts Priscilla had planted.

"Mrs. Banks loves Katherine. And Kenny will, too, once he gets to know her."

It popped out of Merline's mouth before she had a chance to stop herself. She hadn't wanted to give Priscilla the satisfaction of a reply, but she couldn't help it. She wanted to wipe the self-satisfied smirk off the woman's face.

Priscilla frowned but was not cowed. "Yes, I've noticed that Nancy seems to have taken the girl under her wing. She's a charitable woman, so of course she feels sorry for the girl."

Merline recognized the bluff and smiled. Nancy Banks wasn't the type to feel sorry for anyone—she certainly hadn't taken any pity on her. If there was one thing she was sure of, it was that the only reason Nancy had hired her was to keep her grandchild close. Priscilla might be rich and educated, but she didn't know Nancy Banks.

"Soon, she'll have a legitimate grandchild to focus on," Priscilla said triumphantly.

Merline's smile disappeared. She watched Priscilla's hand as it rubbed her still-flat belly.

"I'm due in May," she said, watching Merline's reaction. "I'm going to announce it tomorrow at Christmas dinner—think of it as my Christmas gift to my husband."

She stepped closer and spoke in a low, conspiratorial voice. "It's going to be a boy. I can feel it."

On Christmas Day, Merline arose before the sun and went for a walk. She had begun taking walks just a few days before, after Kenny returned home. With he and Priscilla now living in the Banks home (just until they found their own place, according to Priscilla), Merline now found the enormous home claustrophobic. The past and the future seemed to haunt her at every turn, memories mocking her with their sweetness, uncertainties causing dread in the pit of her stomach.

She walked during the early-morning hours when it was too dark for the white neighborhood to notice a lone black woman wandering its roads. The grand estates were far enough apart so their owners saw each other only when they wanted to. Vast lawns and forest-like gardens ensured privacy, and Merline thought of the homes as hideaways where secret lives were lived, including her own. During these walks, she did not allow herself to dwell on her own failures and regrets. Instead, she spent her walks constructing elaborate fantasies about the lives lived behind the walls of the homes she passed.

She knew some of the women who worked in these houses, Negro women like herself who cooked and cleaned, whose days were spent satisfying the needs of others. They were not her friends, because Merline did not have friends. When she saw them at the market or in town, she nodded politely but spoke little. Most of them were mothers, but none, she noted, had children that were as fair as Katherine. This set her apart, because they all knew her secrets but pretended not to. She believed they both judged and pitied her, feeling sorry for her loneliness, but believing she had reaped what she had sown.

These other maids did not figure into Merline's walking fantasies. What fascinated her was the apparent ease with which the wealthy whites lived, and she liked to imagine being one of them, her skin lightened and her hair straightened. She imagined herself as the lady of the house, with soft, pampered hands and a delicate constitution that made doing chores unthinkable. Her imaginary wardrobe had pink and white suits with matching hats and gloves, formal gowns, delicate slippers and, of course, jewelry for every occasion. The imaginary Merline was called Maria, a name that sounded slightly exotic to her. Maria was young, had just turned twenty-one, in fact. She had celebrated with a grand ball held in

Dallas. Maria wasn't yet married; she had so many wealthy and handsome suitors that it was difficult to choose among them. In any case, Maria had no need to rush into marriage because she had inherited millions from an elderly aunt, and she owned her estate outright. Maria had her entire future ahead of her.

Merline walked for an hour, and as she approached the Banks home, her mood darkened. She was not looking forward to the rest of the day. Nancy had given her the day off—to get her out of the way, Merline suspected—but she had nowhere to go.

She wondered how Mother would spend the holiday, also wondering whether the hard-hearted woman had forgiven her after all these years. She thought about Duck, who had been up in Chicago for five years now. What had become of her? Did she ever think about the sister she'd left behind? For a moment, Merline entertained the idea that she too could run, go to a new place, start a new life.

But there was nowhere, neither close nor far, for Merline to go. She would likely spend the day in her room listening to carols on the radio. In an hour, Katherine would politely accept her gift from Merline, this year an expensive silver mirror, comb, and brush set. She would thank Merline and put the gift aside, unwilling to spend time admiring the intricacy of its design, uninterested in how much time her mother had spent trying to pick the perfect present.

Katherine would be eager to join Nancy, Kenny, and Priscilla in the family room, where she would spend the morning opening a pile of gifts from Nancy. Priscilla would pretend to like her, and after Katherine had opened her gifts, she would announce that she had a special gift for her husband. She would tell him about the baby she was carrying. They would all celebrate by drinking eggnog, even Katherine, who was allowed a small sip by Nancy, even though the drink was spiked with rum.

Kenny would be delighted to become a father. Priscilla would be smug in the knowledge that her baby would put Katherine and Merline in the background where they belonged. Nancy would imagine herself caring for the baby, with help from Katherine. It would be another chance for her to teach her granddaughter what it meant to be a lady.

No one would think about Merline.

In January of 1954, Priscilla had the first of three miscarriages. Eighteen months later, the doctor told her she would never have children, and a devastated Priscilla went into a deep depression that lingered throughout the summer of 1955.

During this time, Merline dealt with her brand of sadness. She saw how the news crushed Kenny, and despite the fact that he had treated Merline with a polite civility that made her wince, she wanted him to be happy.

One hot night in August, Nancy announced at dinner that Katherine, now twelve years old, would be going to an exclusive girls' school beginning that fall. In an uncharacteristic act of kindness, she had asked Merline earlier in the week if she would allow Katherine this opportunity.

"She'll be able to reach her full potential," Nancy had said delicately.

Merline had not wanted to let her daughter go. She read between the lines of Nancy's words. She wasn't worldly, but she'd never heard of a boarding school for rich *Negro* girls, and Nancy must have been talking about sending blonde-haired, green-eyed Katherine as a white girl.

"I'll be her official guardian," Nancy had added, leaving no doubt as to her true intentions.

Merline wanted to say no, that it wasn't right. It might not be fair that Katherine had been born a Negro, but it was true, and she didn't want her to live a lie. She said this to Nancy, who looked at her with genuine sympathy.

"Merline, she's already doing just that. Let her go."

And so, Katherine was going away to Boston. As she served dinner and cleared dishes that August evening, Merline watched and listened carefully. She expected Priscilla to be overjoyed, but nothing could cut through the fog of her depression.

Late that night, Merline heard a soft knock on her door. She looked at Katherine, who was sleeping soundly, then she crept to the door.

"Can we talk?" Kenny whispered.

After gazing at him for a long moment, she pulled on her robe and followed him out to the back garden.

The air was still and moist, fragrant with the smell of hibiscus flowers in bloom. Kenny led her to a cedar bench underneath a Texas oak. Though it was a hot, humid night, Merline felt a chill and pulled her robe more tightly around her. Sitting there with Kenny conjured up a memory of them as children, sitting in the makeshift "parlor" she'd created in the woods, drinking iced tea and talking about the world. It took her back to those simple days, when she and Kenny were innocent and pure.

They sat in silence for a long time, listening to the crickets. She stole a glance at Kenny and wondered if he, too, remembered those childhood nights the same way she did.

"I'm sorry," he said.

"I wasn't asleep, anyway," she said, pretending that he was apologizing for waking her.

He took her hand in his, and their fingers entwined automatically.

"No. I'm sorry for everything. For not being stronger when I was seventeen. For not writing to you. For the past two years, treating you like household help. I'm sorry."

Merline took a deep breath, and when their eyes met, she forgave him. He pulled her close and she could smell the vaguely citrus scent that had always been a part of him.

"I missed you, Merl." He kissed her, and one kiss turned into many, and without thought for anything but herself, Merline made love to Kenny, right there underneath the oak tree in the back garden. Lying in his arms, for the first time in what felt like an eternity, Merline was happy.

In the following days, Katherine packed for boarding school, talking excitedly about all the school brochures she'd read, telling her mother about the friends she would make. Merline watched her daughter with a tightness in her chest. She was glad to see Katherine so vibrant and excited. She was happy for her daughter to have an opportunity to be educated, to be free. But these things did not come free, Merline knew. But she remained silent and hoped that the costs her daughter paid would not be too high.

During this time, Kenny's wife brooded, Kenny's mother invented a new past for Katherine, and life went on. Merline and Kenny took Nancy and Katherine to the Dallas Amtrak station, where they would board a Boston-bound train.

Waving goodbye, Merline knew she was losing her daughter, maybe forever.

But now, she had Kenny.

She had not been forced to choose between Katherine and Kenny—circumstances had chosen for her. She speculated as to what might have happened had she been given the choice.

CHAPTER 12

"A Sunday Kind of Love"

Violet
Greenville, 1947

Violet was thirty-eight years old when she met Rollins, but she looked and felt like a much older woman. She was brutally honest when she looked at herself in the mirror. Years of cleaning houses had given her rough hands and bad knees that cracked when she bent them. After Gray died, she'd stopped caring about what she ate and how she looked, and although there was still evidence of beauty in her face, her body was plump and the shapeless, dark-colored shifts she wore all day did nothing to flatter. She wore no jewelry and didn't bother to style her hair, even when she wasn't wearing her work kerchief.

The strain of working and being the only parent to two daughters showed in the permanent frown line on her forehead, the dark circles under her eyes, the drawn expression on her face. She had done the best she could for the girls. Merline was her favorite because she reminded her of Gray. He would have been happy to see her grow into a lovely young woman, but her mother just worried that beauty would make her daughter vulnerable. Beauty hadn't saved her from a broken heart, so she tried to keep the headstrong Merline under control, forbidding her to wear lipstick, telling her to stay away from charming young men who would someday, one way or another, leave her.

Violet could not bring herself to love her younger daughter, because she reminded her of her own weakness, of the man she'd met in Sonny's. She didn't know his name and she didn't care. He had left her with a baby she didn't want, a reminder that she could never let down her guard. She hardly remembered what the man looked like, but Violet saw neither her grandmother nor her mother in the girl, so she assumed that the baby looked like the man from Sonny's. Dark skin, wide nose, skinny body. It was easy to withhold her love from an ugly baby, and that is what she did until her lack of affection for Duck became a habit.

At seventeen, Merline became secretive. Violet knew something was going on, but she was afraid to know what was making her daughter's cheeks flushed and her eyes secretive. And then the whispers began, and Violet learned that Merline had done what had been forbidden, and with a white man at that. White men had killed Merline's own father, had robbed her mother of the life that was rightfully hers. She simply couldn't understand how Merline could let a white man touch her. Hadn't she been listening to her mother? Didn't she understand that white men were poison?

A black fury had come over her, and she had banished Merline from her life. Violet could not stand to lose anyone else, and now, her eldest daughter was pregnant with a baby that she might grow to cherish. No.

Later, she thought she might have been wrong to send Merline away. After she was gone, Violet and Duck were left alone, and somehow, sharing space with her younger daughter made Violet feel lonelier than she would have on her own. She didn't understand the girl, who spent hours on her own reading and singing when she thought Violet couldn't hear her. Duck seemed to live in a world inside herself, self-contained and independent. She cooked her own meals, kept her room tidier than any teenager should, and she believed in the future in a way that Violet knew was dangerous.

In her own way, she tried to make the girl understand that hopes and dreams were dangerous, but Duck just gave her a blank look and went back into her room. When she lay in her bed alone and unable to sleep, listening to the unnatural silence of the house, Violet sometimes wondered if she had been wrong. Maybe if she had let herself love Merline and Duck, they would have been different. Maybe *she* would have been different, a better self. She tried to imagine herself as one of those mothers who hugged her children when they felt sad, who read them stories before bedtime. She tried to imagine herself as the kind of mother Phoebe was, the kind of person who opened herself up to the world and took the good and the bad in stride. But she couldn't even remember exactly how Phoebe looked, couldn't put herself inside Phoebe's head to understand how she could love with abandon when love caused the worst pain imaginable.

She had done the best she could, Violet told herself on those long sleepless nights. She repeated this to herself, silently, until sleep finally came.

Rollins had made her laugh.

There was a group of men and women who had all taken a well-paying temporary job preparing a newly renovated house for occupancy. The women worked inside, sweeping up sawdust, shining cloudy windows, scouring the insides or porcelain tubs and sinks. The men worked outside, raking leaves, painting, clearing weeds. They all sat together at lunch, flirting and joking while eating the food they'd brought in brown paper bags.

Violet always sat a little bit apart from the group, and early on, they'd all realized that any attempts to get more than brief, non-informative answers to their questions were futile. The women thought she was standoffish, putting on airs. The men thought she was a cold fish, pretty but difficult, not worth the effort. Eventually, they all ignored her and talked amongst themselves. A lot of their talk centered around popular radio shows or local gossip. Once, a man played an old guitar while the others sang silly songs. On the last day of the job, the mood at lunchtime was celebratory, and the women started dancing. The men joined them, and soon the backyard was filled with the sounds of singing, dancing, and laughing.

She watched for a while, taking small bites of her sandwich and thinking of the chores she had to complete before the end of the day. Most of the women were younger than Violet and their enthusiasm for life meant nothing to her. She had found peace with her life, preferred its dullness to the raw pain of her younger years. She was gazing off into nearby trees when Rollins approached.

"Excuse me, madam. May I have this dance?"

He was a round-bodied man about her age, with gray flecks in his close-cropped hair and a sly smile. She glanced over at the others, who had stopped a small distance away to watch. The guitar player was the only one not staring. His eyes closed, he picked out notes to a slow ballad.

"I don't dance." Violet gave him one of her looks, a frown warning him that she was not one to be charmed.

"But please, Miss Violet. You always sit over here by yourself, and I'd just like to have one dance before we part ways and never see each other again."

He had a formal way of speaking that showed he'd had some education in the past.

"I. Don't. Dance." Most people usually left her alone when she used this tone, but Rollins stepped closer and sat next to her on the grass.

"They bet me ten dollars I couldn't get you to dance," he whispered in her ear. "They called it a sucker's bet, said you'd never dance, no matter what. Come dance with me, Miss Violet, and I'll split the money with you."

He leaned back and winked at her. And Violet, in spite of herself, laughed. She laughed longer and harder than she had laughed in many years. It felt good to laugh, as if it released something caught inside her for too long.

She saw the surprise on the others' faces when she took Rollins's outstretched hand, stood up straight and proper, and proceeded to follow his lead in a waltz. She still felt old and tired, but as she danced, her spirit felt a little lighter.

Rollins gave her the five dollars right there in front of everyone, and at the end of the day, he offered to walk her all the way home. She agreed, and for the first time since Gray, she found a man that she liked talking to. When he was around, the house seemed bigger, less lonely. Rollins understood that she would never love him, and it was nice to fall asleep in a man's arms again. He distracted her from regrets, from disappointment, from guilt. They had fun together, and it was enough for him. It was enough for Violet.

Certainly, Rollins had his faults, but he was generally a good man. And that is why she didn't believe Duck when she said he was up to no good in her room at night. No, Violet was a survivor, and her instincts would have told her if Rollins was some kind of pervert. Duck was just mistaken. She didn't know much about men, Violet reasoned. She had misunderstood Rollins's attempts at fatherly affection.

When Duck left, Violet told herself it was for the best. She had been on her own since she was Duck's age, and she had managed. Duck would find her way, too.

CHAPTER 13

"Heartbreak Hotel"

Delia
Chicago, 1952–1956

The first time I sang for an audience, I wasn't aware of the smoke in the air, people shifting in their seats, the clinking of glasses and muted conversations throughout the room. All I could hear was the sound of my heartbeat pounding in my ears. All I could feel was the clammy dampness on my palms. All I could see were shadows and reflections, representations of people sitting and waiting for me to start. My dress was a long white number that swept around my ankles just above the impossibly tall heels I wore. I realized, standing there on stage instead of cleaning bathrooms, that I had never worn heels before. My face felt tight, as if the makeup I was wearing was a mask to hide me from the world. I was never more scared—not of Rollins, not of living on my own in a strange city, not of Marvin Whitman.

I stood there for a moment that felt like years, wondering why I had ever wanted this, when being the center of attention was so excruciating. I suddenly thought this was all wrong; I was Duck, no one special, the one who was either made fun of or ignored. I wasn't Delia, a woman wearing borrowed diamonds in her ears and an expensive wig on her head.

I glanced over to the side of the stage, thinking that I could kick off my shoes and run away, start over again, try to get it right next time. Then I saw Francis. He wore a tuxedo, his hair brushed back elegantly. He nodded encouragement and smiled at me, and I took a deep breath. I owed Francis. He had saved me. He had given me this opportunity to do what I'd always wished for, and to turn my back now would be like turning my back on him. I searched his face for any doubt, and when I found only his sweet, dimpled smile, I turned back to the audience, trying to ignore my stage fright.

That first night in 1952, I sang two songs to the early crowd at Club Royale, serving as an opening act for a sedate crowd who arrived too early to see the headliners, who liked to talk about going to hear jazz more than they actually cared about the music. I sang even though most people were more interested in their drinks. The microphone slipped around in my hands so much, I returned it to the low stand and had to lean over to make sure my voice was heard.

The applause was the kind of polite, dutiful clapping that people offer when they haven't paid much attention to the person on stage. I was insulted and relieved; my first time on stage deserved more, but polite applause was better than none at all.

From then on, I relied on Francis's encouragement to help me avoid being crippled by stage fright.

"It will get easier," he told me. "Everyone gets stage fright, and the important thing is that you don't let it keep you from what you love."

But it didn't get easier. Every time Francis set me up with a gig at the Royale or other smaller venues, I felt that same clamminess, the same fear of disappointing the crowd, the same suspicion that I wasn't a good enough singer, the same feeling that I wasn't pretty enough or charming enough to interest an audience.

I tried to explain to Francis how it felt being on stage. It was Monday morning in June. We had brunch together on days when I wasn't singing, and it was warm and breezy enough for us to find a café with outdoor tables. Francis drank black coffee, as usual, and I drank hot tea with honey to soothe my throat.

"It's as if I stole something, like I'm an imposter and any minute, the audience will realize this and boo me off the stage."

Francis looked surprised. "You've been singing for a year now, and you're pulling good crowds every night. People like your singing, Delia. They wouldn't keep coming back if they didn't."

I was unconvinced. "They come because I sing at your club. People think that becoming regulars on Tuesday nights might help them get tickets to see the real musicians and singers who play here on Friday and Saturday nights."

Francis was silent for a long while, looking out onto the street where passersby seemed to glide by wearing their best summer dresses and linen suits. When he finally turned back to me, his eyes were sad.

"I wanted your dreams to come true. You have a beautiful voice and a lovely face. Why is it so hard for you to believe that?"

I didn't know how to explain to him that deep inside, I would always be Duck.

"Well, look how I got this job. It wasn't because of my singing, was it?"

Francis frowned, as he always did whenever we came close to discussing the connection between Marvin and the singing gigs.

"I gave you the opportunity to sing because you're good."

"And you felt guilty."

He didn't answer. We sat sipping our drinks and ignoring the plates of food in front of us. We gazed in different directions until it was time to pay the bill. Laying cash on the table, Francis stood and took my hand.

"Some day, Delia, you're going to understand how special you are. Yes, I felt guilty after Marvin hurt you. But there were a thousand other ways I could have helped you and made myself feel less guilty along the way."

We walked to his car and he stopped talking. Once inside the car, he continued.

"Damn it, Delia, you're up on stage because you're good. No amount of manipulation on my part can make people like your singing."

His words came out quick and intense. I nodded to placate him, but I still had a knot in my stomach just thinking about singing in front of an audience. He didn't understand how it was to be the ugly duckling. He grew up rich and beautiful, and when life handed him troubles, he always had that to fall back on. Money and beauty could take you a long way in this world, and only someone who had neither could truly understand that. The gulf between me and Francis seemed as if it would never be crossed. Thinking of Marvin Whitman and Kenny Banks, I thought that gulf might well be for the best.

After he spoke, Francis gave me a long look, waiting for me to respond. I couldn't. Finally, he turned his attention to the road ahead.

Acting as my manager, Francis made sure that my career had legs. He booked me each week, and as my name and voice became more well-known around Chicago, he moved me from the slow nights to the best slots each week.

Despite my struggles with stage fright and self-doubt, I eventually came to accept that I was good. My alto voice was husky and deep, and I could hold a note long enough to make the audience explode in applause before I moved on to the next.

I was good, but never great. At first, I only sang at the Royale, but soon, other clubs around Chicago wanted to book me and Francis encouraged me. After I got out of the hospital, we formed an unlikely friendship. I stopped being afraid to speak my mind to him, and I never thought about color when we were alone together. It was the first time I had realized that it was possible for blacks and whites to really be friends, even if, in the nineteen-fifties, it was a tricky proposition.

"You should go to New York, Kansas City, even Los Angeles. Spread your wings a little, see what's out there," Francis told me after I had a successful few years singing in Chicago.

No, I told him. I didn't want to leave Chicago. It finally felt like home. I had grown accustomed to the frozen winters and the humid summers. I now had my own apartment and enough money to take a cab when the cold bit too hard or the heat sizzled the sidewalks. I had a record player and a collection of my favorite records. I had bookshelves full of books that were mine to keep. Most times when I looked in the mirror, I no longer saw an awkward girl named Duck. I saw Delia Dukes, a singer with a following and a future. Duck returned only in those moments when I stood under the spotlight on a stage.

What I didn't admit to Francis then was that I didn't want to leave him, either. There was nothing romantic between us, and that was okay because I couldn't imagine a world in which Francis Whitman would romance Duck Dukes. I had my singing to keep me company. And I had Francis. He showed me the world and I eagerly took it all in. He talked about music, of course, but he also loved books. He didn't think it was odd that on my nights off, I'd rather sit home and read Richard Wright, William Faulkner. I loved Flannery O'Connor.

"Her stories remind me a little of Texas. She's from the South, too. She understood how horrible and lovely it could be at the same time," I explained to Francis one evening. He had convinced me to come to his house for dinner for the first time, and I had been reluctant to accept. He badgered me until I gave in, teasing him that his neighbors would think he was hiring a new maid.

"You should read Gwendolyn Brooks. She's from Chicago, won the Pulitzer in 1950."

I laughed. "You mean I never told you the story of how I picked Chicago as my new home?" Of course, I knew I had never told him any of it. In a way, I wanted him to think of me as Delia Duke, not Duck. I didn't want him to know about my family and how things had been back in Greenville. I wasn't sure how to explain Mother, who had never been much of a mother to me.

"You never told me much about your past."

I looked away, sipping at my wine.

"Delia, everyone has a past. I want to know about yours. I want to know everything about you," he said gently. "We're friends. Friends share secrets."

I looked at him. We already shared secrets—about Marvin and what he had done to me. Nothing I could tell him about my childhood could be worse than that.

So I told him everything. I told him about Mother, about Rollins, about Merline, Kenny, and Katherine. I told him about the sign in Greenville, "The Blackest Land, The Whitest People." And afterward, I realized that Francis was the only person who really knew me. He was the first true friend I ever had, and that gulf between us shrank a bit each day.

I met Christopher on New Year's Eve, 1953. We were both on a variety bill at the biggest club in Chicago that featured singers, cabaret dancers, and musicians. I had never had a gig this big, though I was near the bottom of the bill with a few other regional acts with little national presence.

Christopher and I were the same age, twenty-three, but he carried himself like a much older, mature man. He played the violin, which was a choice almost unheard of for a jazz musician. He was the show's top act, a position anyone but the most experienced and famous would envy. He would face a crowd that was still talking and ordering drinks, but I'd seen singers and musicians overcome that early-evening indifference with one well-chosen note. Christopher seemed capable of grabbing people's attention and holding on to it until *he* was ready to let go.

He was small and lean and his butterscotch skin was smooth and unblemished, except for a raised scar that ran from the right side of his jaw down to his collarbone. The collar of his crisp white shirts hid most of it, and he never told anyone the truth about how he'd gotten it. Instead, he told each person (each woman, since the women were the ones who were interested in Christopher) a different story during rehearsals. His eyes were wide, with long lashes that made him look almost childlike, especially when he widened them when telling one of his stories about the scar. I was in the room when he told another singer that he'd been stabbed by a junkie one night in Harlem. He gave enough details to keep the woman rapt, but I rolled my eyes when I thought he couldn't see me.

Christopher was nothing but trouble, a charming liar who will say anything to get a woman's attention.

I'd had a series of brief physical relationships with trumpeters and pianists and be-bop princes who were charming and fun. But I never let them get too close to me, and they were sometimes confused by the fact that when they were ready to leave me, I was just as ready for them to go. Christopher, despite his sinewy good looks and his alien violin, didn't seem like the type to fade away, so I kept my distance.

I went about my business as he finished describing the junkie's knife in lurid detail. When he was finished, his companion cooed over his misfortune, taking the opportunity to sit closer to him and lay sympathetic hands on him. I shook my head, thinking of how easily some people were fooled. Christopher looked up at me and winked as the woman looked through her purse for a pen to write down her telephone number.

I couldn't help laughing. A chuckle escaped my lips, followed by more laughter at the amused look on Christopher's face. The other woman's lips tightened suspiciously. Then Christopher started to laugh, and by the time his admirer stomped out of the room, we were both doubled over.

"That scar is probably the best thing that ever happened to you. Without it, how would you meet women?" I asked after our giggling had subsided.

He raised one sandy eyebrow, which matched his close-cropped reddish hair. "And here I thought they were all interested in my charm and talent as a violinist."

"The violin is a plus, but without the scar, you're just a cute guy who plays an instrument most of them have never heard."

He gave me a slow smile. "So you think I'm cute."

I felt my cheeks get hot. "Not as cute as you think you are."

I left then, the twinkling sound of his laughter following me out the door.

At the show that night, I hid in the shadows off stage and watched Christopher play. He closed his eyes and gently drew the bow back and forth over the strings, creating sounds that blended the best of jazz and classical music into something completely new. His tuxedo fit his trim body perfectly, and he managed to be intense and at ease at the same time. He was left-handed, so when he played, the scar disappeared and took with it the cocky attitude he'd displayed during rehearsals. Now he was just a man in love with music.

When he finished, I hurried backstage while he took his bows. I didn't want him to know I'd been watching.

When it was my turn, he watched as I took my place at the microphone behind the closed curtain. I barely noticed him as I went through my usual routine while waiting for the curtain to open. My clammy hands shook, beads of sweat formed at my brow, and I wrestled with the idea that I was a fraud in a dress and heels. I took my last deep breath as my name was announced over the loudspeaker. Once I sang the first note, I could focus on the words and the melody instead of myself. Polite applause carried me backstage, where I sat down, slipped off my shoes, closed my eyes and tried to slow my heartbeat.

"Does that happen every time?" Christopher had taken the seat next to me on a worn loveseat. He smelled of cigarettes and a slightly sweet cologne that smelled like a forest just after a rain.

I looked at him, alert. Francis is the only person I had talked to about my stage fright, and even he couldn't really understand. Christopher seemed like someone who always got what he wanted. Life was easier for men, even black men, especially those with Christopher's charm and grace. He wouldn't understand.

"Does *what* happen?"

He was silent for a moment, his eyes on mine. I held his gaze, pretending a boldness I didn't feel.

"I used to have the jitters way back when I first started out," he said. Until that moment, his voice had sounded like every Chicago native I knew—nasal, clipped, quick. But a drawl crept into his voice when he said "jitters," as if he came from somewhere far south, just like me.

"Way back? You can't be more than nineteen, maybe twenty," I teased, trying to change the subject.

He didn't take the bait. "I'm twenty-three, but I've been on my own since I was twelve. And those jitters used to really get me."

"Jitters? They sound awful. But I don't have anything like that," I lied.

He gave me his long stare again, and I felt as if he was reading my mind. I stared back, trying to erase the truth from my face.

"Where are you from?" he asked.

I was thrown off. "Texas. Greenville."

He nodded. "I'm from Houston. Haven't been back in a long time, but I recognized your accent."

I smiled, happy to find someone who knew Texas and pleased that we were no longer talking about my jitters.

He rose from the small sofa, his hand brushing mine. I had been right about his skin; the tops of his hands were velvety, as if he'd never done a bit of hard work in his life. The calluses on his palms attested to his hours of practice, gripping the violin in one hand and the bow in the other.

He put his hands in his pockets and looked down at me. "Delia Dukes from Greenville, Texas, if you ever want some help with those jitters, you give Chris Langston from Houston, Texas, a call." He said this in a deep drawl with a smile on his face. From his pocket he drew a white calling card with his name and telephone number on it. He handed it to me and left.

For the first time since my singing career began, I stood on stage feeling a sense of lightheaded peace. My arms felt soft, almost boneless. The tension in my shoulders had disappeared, and at that moment, I believed it would never return. My legs felt limber, and I leaned to one side with my hand on my hip, a stance I had never attempted on stage. Before, I stood straight, looking at a spot just beyond the faces watching me. Now, I roamed the stage holding the microphone in my hand, making eye contact with regulars who seemed to be noticing me for the first time, though I had sung for them many times before. My eyelids were pleasantly heavy, my smile felt sultry instead of strained.

I was booked for three songs, serving as the opening act for a band from Los Angeles that was playing in a cool, lazy style that Chicago audiences were starting to love. Some nights, a three-song set lasted an eternity. Tonight, I received the most enthusiastic applause of my career.

For the first time in two years, I felt as if I belonged on stage, in this world of sensual singers, charming saxophonists and witty pianists. I was a part of this nocturnal Eden, where days were spent waiting for darkness to fall so we could get on with the business of music. I was no long Duck. I was Delia.

Christopher was waiting for me when I finished my set.

"Look at you, Dame Delia," he said with a slow grin. "I told you I could help you with those jitters."

I laughed, still high, though we'd smoked hours before I went on.

"I never should have doubted you."

"Never doubt me, Delia." His voice was slow, a drawl that hinted at his Texas roots. "I will always have what you need."

He looked at me, his eyes filled with the meaning of his words. I returned his gaze, feeling an undercurrent of attraction between us.

"How about dinner?" he asked.

"And after dinner?"

I expected him to laugh, but his face remained serious.

"Like I said, I'll give you what you need."

Letting Christopher into my bed felt like the most natural thing in the world. He was funny and liked to make up nicknames for me that made me blush. Back home in Greenville, being Duck felt like a prison sentence. But Christopher had never known me as Duck. To him, I was Dame Delia, Delightful, and, when we were alone in his apartment or mine, Delicious.

We never talked about the past. We were simply the people we chose to be at that moment, and nothing else mattered. Sometimes I wondered when he'd left Texas and why, what his family was like, how he learned to play the violin. But asking questions would have ruined what we had: a love affair with no before, no after, just the present.

I thought of Christopher as both a lover and a friend. In my mind, Francis didn't count. Though he protested,

I still secretly feared that our friendship was based on obligation. He felt he owed me because of what his brother had done, because I was a poor black girl with no family and no roots, because he was too nice to leave me to fend for myself.

I truly believed that about Francis. Christopher was his polar opposite. He liked the Delia standing right in front of him. He didn't see me as damaged. He wasn't particularly charitable and was not the type to even notice a person in need. He was all about pleasure: Christopher lived to feel good, and for the first time in my life, I let myself be free to do the same, both offstage and on.

Christopher's miracle cure for my stage fright came in the form of slim, hand-rolled cigarettes that contained a sweet, pungent weed that blurred the edges of reality. Christopher was unpredictable, and I never knew whether he would come to see me sing, or whether he would be mysteriously absent for a week. But even when he was not there in person, he made sure I had a steady supply of what he called my "medicine." I took it faithfully, and for a while, it helped. I booked more gigs, the applause seemed louder and my voice was often husky and raw, giving a new edge to my songs.

Francis disapproved. As my manager, he appeared at all my gigs, making sure the microphones were working, that the piano players knew the set list, that I was ready to go onstage. In March of 1954, about a month after Christopher introduced me to his magical cure, Francis became worried about me.

I was back at the Club Royale for a weeklong engagement. Though I saw Francis often, I no longer spent all my free time with him. I no longer confided in him about my past, having seen the fun of living in the present, and he noticed that I was no longer petrified before each performance.

I was putting the final touches on my makeup and humming to myself when Francis knocked on the dressing room door and asked to come in. I smiled lazily at his reflection in the vast wall mirror.

"You seem different lately," he said, not returning my smile.

I focused on making the lipstick in my hand meet my lips. This struck me as funny and I couldn't help giggling. The stern look on his face only made me laugh harder.

"What is going on with you?"

"What is going on with *you*?" I repeated, mocking his fatherly tone.

Francis grabbed my shoulder and turned me around to face him.

"Delia, it's me. Talk to me."

My reflexes slowed, I was annoyed that Francis was getting in the way of my high.

"I'm on in five minutes. I should get ready."

Francis shook his head. "I'm the owner—we can take our time." He paused, as if he didn't want to ask his next question.

"Are you on something?"

I shook his hand off my shoulder and turned back to the mirror.

"Francis, you sound so square when you say that."

"Well, are you?"

I sighed, looking away from the intensity of his gaze reflected in the mirror.

"I just need a little help with the jitters, that's all. I've got some medicine now. It helps me."

Francis knitted his eyebrows, his lips pursed into a tight line.

"Marijuana is not medicine. Who gave it to you? It was that Christopher, wasn't it?"

I took my time sweeping blush over my cheekbones, making him wait. When I looked up at him, he seemed as if he'd aged ten years since walking through the dressing room door.

"You are not my big brother. You are not my father," I continued, smiling as he winced. He was just seven years older than me, but I knew he was sensitive about his age. I had hit my target.

"I'm a big girl, Francis. I can take care of myself."

I stood, straightened my gown and left him standing there, ignoring the small, faint voice in my head that told me to stay, apologize, talk to the first and only true friend I'd ever had.

We were both a part of the music world, but I soon realized that Christopher's love affair with his violin, his attachment to his art, was much deeper than anything I'd ever felt. I liked to sing, to escape from my life into the fantasy of a song. I had a good voice—not great, but good. Christopher drew his bow over strings as if he were caressing a woman's body. Sometimes, as we lay together in bed, he hummed an unfamiliar melody. When he slept, he sang lyrics to that same melody, but it was no song I'd ever heard.

"It exists only inside my head," he told me when I asked. "I could say I wrote it, but that wouldn't be quite the truth. It came to me in a dream. It lives beyond me, and although I give it life with my voice, it's not truly mine."

Sometimes Christopher said things that confused me and made me feel small. He seemed to experience music in a completely different way from me. I was using music; the music, he told me, used him.

With Christopher, I discovered a Chicago I had never known. I had never had much time to explore the city; when I first arrived from Greenville, my life was about work and survival. When I began singing, I spent nights in clubs and days sleeping. Christopher lived in the same nighttime world as I did, but he slept only a few hours during the day, and when we were together, I adopted the same routine. We walked all over the city, ignoring the stares when we ventured into white neighborhoods, ignoring the catcalls when we reached the South Side.

One sunny Saturday afternoon in May, we took advantage of unseasonable warmth and headed to Grant

Park for a midday picnic. Christopher led me around the park, trying to find the perfect shady spot with a view of Lake Michigan. I followed, docile and yawning, having slept only three hours before his urgent knocking at my door woke me.

When we finally found a place he deemed acceptable, we spread out a blanket and unpacked the food. Christopher had prepared the picnic, and I expected something simple, maybe sandwiches from a deli and lemonade. My mouth dropped open as he set up a feast of roasted chicken, homemade potato salad, three different kinds of cheeses, fresh French bread and two bottles of wine.

"I wasn't sure whether you like red or white," he said apologetically, as if he thought I was staring in judgment of his choices.

"I can't believe all this. Where did it come from?" I was still young and innocent enough to be impressed by a picnic lunch.

Christopher laughed at the amazement on my face. "I made it. Except the wine. I don't have my own vineyard."

"You can cook?"

"Of course." He seemed slightly offended by my question.

"I didn't mean anything bad by that. I've just never known a man who cooks. Not like this." Francis ordered takeout or ate out at restaurants almost every night.

"Who taught you to cook like this?" Even as I spoke I realized that I'd broken the unspoken rule of our relationship: Never talk about the past or the future.

For a moment, our eyes met, and I saw conflicting emotions in his gaze. I had hit a nerve. Whoever taught him to cook had also broken him, made him run to Chicago to become a man with a gift for music and lies. I remembered how many different stories he'd told about his scar, not one of them true. I didn't blame him for not wanting to talk about Texas. We had lived hundreds of miles apart, but I suspected the scar on his neck wasn't the only one he carried with him every day.

Christopher looked away, busying himself with a corkscrew. I knew he wouldn't answer me, but in that moment, I felt desperate to know him better. It was a melancholy longing, one that I knew, even at the peak of our affair, it would never be fulfilled. We were very different, but we had one thing in common: We'd both come to Chicago to escape the past. I had at least told one person—Francis—about mine. I was sure that Christopher had never met anyone he trusted with his secrets, not even me.

A long silence passed. I was still, looking out at the impossibly blue lake, listening to the sounds of cicadas buzzing and Christopher setting out real china and silverware.

"Red or white?" he asked, holding up a bottle in each hand.

The churning emotions were replaced by his usual teasing grin.

"I've never tasted either one. You'd better pick."

He filled two glasses halfway, one with Chardonnay, the other with Burgundy. "Well, then, let's have both."

I took the glass of white first and was about to take a drink. Christopher held up his hand to stop me.

"First, we have to make a toast." He paused, thinking. "Let's toast to new beginnings."

"To new beginnings." I smiled, trying to ignore the voice inside my head warning that where there are beginnings, there must be endings.

By June, I was exhausted from long nights and day-long excursions with Christopher.

"You look terrible," Francis told me one night. He had come into the dressing room after the show, and I was feeling cranky because my highs were sinking, and I hadn't had a good night's sleep in weeks.

"Thanks," I growled. "I guess you're finally seeing me for who I really am. Duck Dukes isn't the pretty one. Never was."

I spat out the words, deliberately using my deepest Texas drawl.

Francis's eyes were sad. "Delia, you are as lovely as always. Except for those dark circles under your eyes."

I looked away, not wanting him to see that his words embarrassed me. Christopher told me all the time that he liked the way I looked, that my dark skin reminded him of ebony, that my lanky frame, wide nose, and high cheekbones were like those of an African queen. But Christopher's words were theatrical, meant to impress and amuse. Francis spoke simply and honestly, and this made me dangerously vulnerable.

"I haven't been sleeping much lately."

"What have you been doing?"

I didn't want to argue with Francis. It was late, I was weary, and I didn't like the way he acted when he saw me with Christopher. He was barely civil, offering only brusque greetings and refusing to meet Christopher's eyes.

"Your big brother doesn't like me much," Christopher liked to tease when he was in a dark mood. I didn't like to be around him during these moods. I could never predict when they would appear, but when they did, Christopher's humor changed from teasing to sarcastic and biting. Whatever distance existed between me and Francis, I was nonetheless always coming to his defense when Christopher mocked him.

"He's just worried about me."

"He acts like a jealous boyfriend," Chris had whined. These dark moods were becoming more frequent, and I couldn't decide which was less attractive: the meanness or the whining tone.

"We're friends. He cares about me."

"Too much."

I had shrugged and changed the subject.

Now, sleep-deprived and irritable, I was once again faced with Francis's concern.

"I've been having fun with Christopher. Why does that bother you so much?"

Francis was silent for a moment, as if weighing his words carefully.

"I don't think he's good for you. He's on who-knows-what kind of dope, he's got you going for days at a time without sleep. If he cared about you, he wouldn't want to see you like this."

I was offended by the implication that I was just a puppet in Christopher's hands.

"He hasn't forced me to do anything," I said, my voice rising to a near scream. "I make my own choices. Me! I am twenty-three, old enough to choose my own friends, Francis."

I stood up, and without thinking, I shoved Francis in his chest. He was taller and stronger than me, so the momentum drew me into his body while he barely moved at all. We stood close, the room suddenly quiet except for the sound of our breathing. Gently, Francis put his arms around me, drawing me closer, and before I knew it, I was sobbing. The lapels of his jacket grew wet from my tears, and when I finally calmed down, Francis led me to his car and drove me home. I fell into my bed, and slept for the next fifteen hours.

I might have slept longer, but the telephone rang so regularly and so persistently until I could no longer ignore it.

"We should go see a movie. *On the Waterfront* is playing."

I looked over at the clock and I couldn't tell if it was four in the morning or night, because my shades were down and my curtains were drawn tight.

"Christopher?"

He gave a manic laugh. "The next showing is at seven. I'll come get you."

"Wait, no. I'm still sleeping. Or I was sleeping."

He started speaking quickly, his words tripping over each other, making it hard for me to follow. What I caught was that the world would pass me by if I slept all day, that he couldn't believe I would rather laze around in bed than go to the theater. Then I could have sworn he said something about Orlando.

"Wait, what? Orlando? In Florida?" My thoughts were fuzzy and disjointed. All I wanted to do was hang up the telephone and lie back down.

"Jesus, Delia. Marlon Brando! I said Brando. I love him. He's perfect in *On the Waterfront.*" He was becoming exasperated, but I was starting to get angry. If anyone should be frustrated, it was me.

"Christopher, I need sleep. I don't know how you do it, staying up all night and day, but I'm off tonight, and all I want to do is sleep some more. And you already saw *On the Waterfront* at least twice."

He gave another manic giggle. "No such thing as too much Brando, baby. Now, that sleeping thing—I have just the cure for that. Remember, I've got what you need."

I frowned, now fully awake. "Smoking will just make me more tired."

"Not smoke, my Darling Delia. This cure comes in a little white pill that will help you stay up forever if you want to."

I thought about Christopher's changing moods, the way he never needed sleep, the way he always had a "cure" for what just seemed like life to me. There was a sour spot in the pit of my stomach.

"The only cure I need is sleep. I'll talk to you tomorrow. You'll be in the band tomorrow night, right?"

I waited for him to answer. The line crackled with static for a long while, and then there was a click followed by a dial tone.

By fall 1954, I had discovered the source of Christopher's changing moods. He sometimes disappeared for days at a time, and he had become increasingly unpredictable and difficult. In early October, two weeks had passed since I had last seen him, and I was worried. I went to his apartment on a Sunday, hoping to find him alive and well, hoping to chastise him for being careless and forgetful, planning to kiss and make up.

I had missed him. And I was eager to share a new revelation. During the two weeks without Christopher's "medicine," I discovered that I no longer needed help with my stage fright. The first two nights without Christopher and his supply, I panicked, thinking I would be paralyzed with fear after so many months of going on stage in a daze. But once I stepped out into the spotlight, I found my voice and the pounding in my chest had subsided by the second verse.

By the end of that first week, I began to suspect that my jitters were gone for good, and after another week without Christopher, I knew I didn't need to be numbed before going onstage. I felt stronger, more confident, and I thought Christopher would be as happy as Francis had been when I told him.

I rang the doorbell, then pounded my fist on the door. I was just about to give up and leave when I heard the sound of feet shuffling, and the door opened just a crack.

I had never seen Christopher like this. His eyes were bloodshot, his skin looked dry, and he smelled as if he hadn't bathed since I last saw him.

"What?"

At first I smiled, thinking his sullen greeting was a joke. But his expression didn't change.

"Christopher, I've been worried about you."

He coughed, a phlegmy sound that rattled through his chest.

"Are you okay?"

"I'm just taking your advice. Getting more sleep. 'That's the only cure I need,' right?"

He had never used this biting, nasty tone with me, and I didn't like the way he mocked my words, lying to me as he'd lied to all those women before we met. He was dressed in pajamas, looking and sounding as if he were gravely ill.

"Christopher, let me in."

"Now, I'm in here tryin' to get mah beauty sleep and you want to come in?" he drawled in a thick Texas accent.

"Please."

He rubbed his eyes, sighed, and let the door swing open. He walked down the hall to his bedroom and slammed the door, making it clear that I was not welcome to follow him. I stood in his living room, taking in the dishes encrusted with moldy food, the ashtrays filled with cigarette butts, the filthy clothing strewn around the room. The curtains were drawn, making it hard to see, and I turned on a lamp. In the sudden brightness my eyes were drawn to a side table, where three items lay in a neat row: a hypodermic needle, a bent, discolored spoon, and some kind of rubber tubing.

As much as I had grown up, as much as Christopher had taught me about Chicago, about music, about Marlon Brando, I had no idea what those three things were for. I just knew that the sight of them made my heart beat faster. I knew that anything that involved needles in the living room had to be bad. I backed away, slowly leaving the apartment and closing the door softly behind me.

The next night, I asked a bass player named Solomon if he knew what the things were for. He was a set musician, affiliated with no one band or singer, and although we'd shared the stage on several occasions, we had never said much to each other beyond basic greetings. He was an older man who wore his salt-and-pepper hair in a processed pompadour. He sported a small mustache and dressed in colorful suits.

"Well, Delia, I didn't think you were that kind of girl. You want to know how to get some black pearl? I don't partake myself, but I can point you in the right direction."

He laughed at the puzzled, worried look on my face.

"No, I didn't think you were the type." He paused, thinking. "You must be asking about your sweetheart, that violin-strummer Chris."

I looked at my toes, feeling somehow ashamed, as if I'd given away a secret, even though I didn't even know what the secret was.

"Why do you think it's about Christopher?"

He must have seen the fear in my eyes, because he stopped teasing. His voice went low and serious.

"Everyone knows that *Christopher* likes his share of tar now and then. He hasn't been around lately, so I'm thinking that now and then has become more like all the time."

Suddenly, something clicked. I'd always heard whispers about dope, and of course, I had smoked my share with Christopher. But this was something else, the kind of thing that kept a man from washing, that made him mean and erratic. This was the kind of thing that made Christopher into a stranger who turned his back on me without thinking twice.

"Can I ask a dumb question? Is he . . . putting it into his body? With the needle, I mean."

The bass player's face grew sad, as if he just realized he'd lost something precious.

"Honey, it's not a dumb question, just innocent. Seems like a lifetime since I was as innocent as you." He reached into his pocket and handed me a crisp white handkerchief. I hadn't even realized I was crying.

"I'm sorry to tell you that your sweetie is using heroin, and yes, he's shooting it into his arm."

I must have looked hopeful, because he shook his head. "If you're thinking of trying to help him, you want to think again. We're not friends, but I've known that boy a lot longer than you, and for as long as I've known him, his true love has been that needle."

"What will happen to him?"

Solomon gazed into the distance, as if the answer was written on the far wall but he couldn't quite read the words.

"Delia, do you have family? No? How about a friend? I mean, a true friend."

I had Francis. Things had gotten better between us, but as long as Christopher was in the picture, I knew Francis would keep his distance from me. Unless I needed him.

"I have a friend."

Solomon sighed. "Go to your friend. Let this other thing go. Be with someone who loves you, not the needle."

He patted me on the shoulder and walked over to where his bass rested in its stand and prepared to practice, picking notes here and there, listening for the right tone.

I thought about what Solomon had said. Maybe he was right, I should go to Francis, tell him what I'd seen, talk it through, ask his advice. Another week passed and Christopher had not returned. He simply did not show up for gigs I knew he'd booked months ago. By Halloween, people had stopped wondering where he was, and club life seemed to move easily past its brief love affair with a young jazz violinist.

I was the only one who had not moved on, and though part of me knew Solomon was right, I believed that I owed Christopher one more chance. Halloween fell on a Sunday that year, and I decided to visit him in the morning, while most people were at church or still asleep.

As I walked up Christopher's block, I saw a police car and an ambulance parked in front of his house. A small crowd had gathered and beat cops were trying to shoo them away. Panic rose in my throat when I saw that the door to Christopher's apartment building was propped open. Official-looking men wandered in and out of the building, lighting and finishing cigarettes with no sense of urgency.

I was already crying by the time I reached the small group of onlookers, and I had to repeat my question twice because the young fair-skinned woman who was nearest to me couldn't understand my words.

"They found somebody dead in there," she said casually, as if she witnessed death every day and talking about it was about as important as talking about the weather. "I live across the street here, so I used to see him around, you know?"

"Who?" I choked on the word, already knowing the answer.

"Don't know his name. I heard the police say he was some kind of a musician, and it sounded like they said 'violin,' but I must have been hearing things, because I have never known any black person who played the violin."

The next day I got up early to get the newspaper from the corner stand, and I read it right there at the newsstand. A brief item in the newspaper reported that a musician named Christopher Langston had died of a heroin overdose.

I walked back to my apartment, the newspaper clutched in my hand. When I reached the stoop, I saw Francis sitting, waiting for me.

CHAPTER 14
"She's a Fool"

Merline
Dallas, 1963

If she heard the whiny "Walk Like a Man" one more time, Merline thought she might be driven to either murder or insanity. Perhaps both. The song could be heard everywhere she went in Dallas—playing in the stores, screaming from car radios, on the lips of passing teenagers. Frankie Valli had annoyed her with a series of ditties over recent months, including the insufferable "Big Girls Don't Cry." Although this might have fit the soundtrack of Merline's life, since she did, in fact, view crying as an activity best left to children and weaklings, Frankie Valli's falsetto still grated on her nerves.

She had never cared much for music, especially since she couldn't sing a lick. When they were children, Duck was the one who always had the radio playing, but for Merline it was just background noise. She preferred listening to the news stations, feeling compelled to keep up with current events ever since Katherine was old enough to make her feel ignorant. Although Katherine was gone, first at boarding school, then college, Merline still lis-

SWAN

tened to the AM talk stations as a part of her daily routine. That routine now included working in the corporate office of Banks Brothers, Inc. She wore A-line skirts, fitted jackets with rounded collars, and, sometimes, if she was feeling particularly lively, a matching pillbox hat.

At thirty-eight years old, Merline was a working woman who traveled each day to an office, where she managed the entire maintenance staff at Banks, Inc. She was independent and self-sufficient. She lived in the city and felt herself more sophisticated than the people she'd left behind in Greenville. She held her head high as she walked around the building Banks, Inc. occupied in downtown Dallas's commercial district. In her mind she had achieved everything the Freedom Riders and the NAACP were demanding. Whites greeted her as Miss Dukes when they passed her in the halls. She had a good job, her own two-bedroom apartment, and if she couldn't vote or sit in some restaurants, well, she didn't really care much about politics or eating out.

Most important, she finally had Kenny. He had come back to her after all those years of waiting and hoping. They were together once again, and they didn't have to sneak around in the woods or worry about their parents' disapproval. Yes, he was still married to Priscilla, and no, Merline didn't get to see Kenny as much as she wanted. Even when they were together, things weren't always perfect. Kenny liked to talk—about work, about movies and, most of all, about politics. He had gone on a rant the day Kennedy was shot, saying that there was no hope for a country that would allow this to happen.

210

"It's a sad thing when a man gets killed. But it seems to me that people will just keep on going, just like they always do," Merline replied.

It was a Sunday night, which Kenny usually spent at home with Priscilla. But his wife had drunk too much red wine and had fallen asleep early. It had been short notice, but Merline cooked a steak and buttery mashed potatoes for Kenny.

They were sitting at her glass-topped dining room table. Kenny stopped chewing and stared at her.

"We're talking about the president of the United States. Not just any man—the man who was poised to change the fate of this country."

"I know that. I'm just saying that things will go on without him, one way or another."

Kenny shook his head. "Don't you care about civil rights? You can't even vote."

Merline shrugged and cut another piece of steak. She knew it would make Kenny mad if she told him that she wouldn't have the slightest idea who to vote for, even if she could. After a few minutes of strained silence, Merline changed the subject to *The Lucy Show*, finally making him laugh by reenacting Lucille Ball's wacky skits. Once he laughed, she relaxed. They had so little time together. She didn't want to waste a moment arguing.

One point of contention between them was Katherine. She had wanted him to get to know his daughter when he returned home back in 1953, but he couldn't figure out a way to balance Priscilla, his mother,

Merline, and Katherine without causing World War III. So he had been like a pleasant but distant uncle to Katherine back then. Now that Katherine was older, Merline wanted him to talk to her, to visit her. It would be okay—he was white and, according to Nancy's invented background, he was connected to Katherine through Nancy. The only truth in Katherine's invented past was the fact that Nancy was her grandmother.

Kenny rebuffed Merline's efforts.

"It's been too long," he said. "I can't just create a relationship with Katherine out of thin air."

She was persistent. "But she needs family, she needs more than just an old woman. I can't go see her. But you can."

"She doesn't even know I'm her father."

"So be her uncle."

Kenny had said he would think about it, but he never brought it up again, and each time Merline broached the subject, they had the same frustrating argument.

Their relationship wasn't perfect, but she had at least a part of him, and she had decided that a little was better than nothing at all. Merline was a realist; life wasn't perfect, and she was going to enjoy hers.

As far as she was concerned, she was free.

Most of the other women who worked for Banks, Inc. were much younger or much older than Merline, who had forbidden her coworkers from doing anything to acknowledge her thirty-eighth birthday earlier that year. There were secretaries in their early twenties who spent their days answering telephones and their evenings on dates with eligible young men, always hoping and searching for the one who would marry them and end their working days for good. At the other end of the spectrum were the older women who were divorced or widowed, women who were pitied as tragic figures because they had to work though they were near retirement age.

What the young and older women had in common was that working at the office was a necessity, not a choice. Merline was unique in that she chose to be unmarried and working. It was what Kenny had to offer, and so she ignored the whispers and snickers. She ignored the whispered rumors that she was a lesbian, a call girl, a spy, a man, a convict, unnatural, weird. No one knew that she and Kenny were lovers. That was a condition of their arrangement, as he was still married to Priscilla and did not want to shame her in front of her society friends.

In exchange for her discretion, Kenny offered an apartment in Dallas, a position at his company and two to three nights a week with him. On most days, Merline believed it was enough.

So she stayed on at Banks, Inc. as, one by one, the older women finally retired and the younger girls married and were replaced by even younger girls. As a matter of etiquette, she was regularly invited to these weddings.

The latest invitation came from a girl named Tate who liked to go around saying she and Merline were friends. She did this because she thought of herself as a progressive, someone who didn't see color, who didn't care about social class. Of course, it was easy for Tate to feign class and racial tolerance, since she was white and was born into a fortune. One day in the lunchroom, where Merline was sitting alone eating a sandwich she'd brought from home, Tate took the empty seat next to her at the table and confided that she worked because she wanted to, not because she had to.

"It builds character," she said. "It's important to give back to the community."

She leaned in and said in a loud whisper, "You know, Daddy gives money to those Freedom Riders over in Alabama and Georgia. Don't tell anyone—it would ruin Daddy's business if anyone found out. He just had to do something for those poor Negroes."

Tate smiled and tossed her blonde ponytail. Merline frowned at the smug look on the girl's face and murmured something that sounded vaguely civil.

"Daddy thinks it isn't proper for someone of our means to work in an office. He does have a point, I suppose, but I told him that I wanted to do it, and that was that."

Tate took Merline's lack of comment as support. On days when she did not go out for lunch, she sat next to her and chattered while Merline pretended to be interested. She wished she could tell Tate what she really thought about the girl's parties, her designer clothes, her rich daddy, her incessant talking. But she was a professional, and telling off Tate would not be proper.

The invitation to Tate's engagement party was just like her: cheery and rich. Her perfect parents requested Merline's presence at their perfect party at the Ritz Carlton. The thick cream paper, the embossed lettering, the smooth script—it all rose up from Merline's desk, mocking her. She knew she'd never have a wedding, not to Kenny. There weren't any more babies in her future. He was still married to Priscilla, and although he said they led separate lives, even had separate bedrooms, he would not divorce her.

"This is the best I have to give," he whispered to Merline on the nights they spent together in her apartment. Most of the time, she accepted her life and believed that, in the long run, things had turned out better than she could have expected. But some nights, she lay awake next to Kenny, listening to the sound of his breathing, wishing that she could have all his nights and days.

Once, she had suggested this to Kenny.

"I love you, Merline. But I can't leave Priscilla. You know she's not well. She needs me."

But she did not believe Priscilla's sickness, which only appeared when Kenny spent more than two nights a week with her. Threatened, Priscilla's symptoms would appear, vague complaints of dizziness and frailty that were probably complete lies. Priscilla might have her problems, but she knew exactly how to manipulate Kenny. Early on, she had tried to hold onto him by getting pregnant, but had miscarried and was never able to carry a baby to term. The miscarriages were at the root of her illness, Kenny claimed.

"I can't blame her. It's a hard thing to face."

Merline wished she could feel sorry for Priscilla, but just the thought of the woman drove her crazy. She was the only thing standing in the way of her and Kenny, and from the look of things, she planned to stay right where she was.

A tiny voice inside her head wondered if Kenny was just making excuses so he could have a proper white wife to take to business dinners while keeping her conveniently tucked away in the background. Merline didn't like this voice, so she ignored it.

However, the wedding invitations weakened her, and each one she opened seemed to mock her. Tate's was lovely, though it wasn't what Merline would have picked. It, too, seemed to speak to her. You are not good enough, it said. You will never be good enough.

Merline dutifully filled out the response card, offering her sincere regrets that she would not be able to attend. She had no intention of being the old maid at a wedding, especially the wedding of someone she didn't really like. The words she wrote looked as if she had written them with her left hand—awkward, larger than normal, crooked.

In December, Katherine graduated early from Northwestern University, where she studied philosophy. Nancy Banks had, of course, paid for everything. By this time, Merline had grown used to the fact that her daughter was no longer hers. As far as the world was concerned, Katherine was a young white woman with an unlimited future.

Katherine did write to Merline—one letter each month. The letters, addressed to Miss Merline Dukes, were filled with tales of sorority parties and girlish enthusiasm. Katherine never referred to her as Mother or Mama. The letters never told Merline what she really wanted to know: Did Katherine feel safer as a white woman? Did anyone ever guess her secret? Didn't she miss her mother, just a little?

When Katherine came home for holidays and school breaks, she and her mother found that they had very little to say to each other. Katherine looked somehow paler and blonder with each visit, and even the way she spoke changed as she adopted the flat Midwestern accent television newscasters used. At the time of her graduation, she had not returned to Texas in two years. Nancy Banks had often visited Katherine at Northwestern, but Merline was never invited along. Of course, it was only proper that she be invited to her daughter's graduation ceremony, but she declined. How would her presence be explained? Would she be the maid? A former nanny? It seemed best for everyone if she stayed away.

A week before Christmas, Nancy visited Merline at her apartment. After Katherine had gone away to school, Nancy had been kinder to Merline. They never spoke about Kenny, about Merline's job at Banks, Inc., about how she afforded the spacious apartment. They only talked about Katherine, either on the telephone, or, rarely, in person. Nancy kept her informed of the girl's activities, and she always made an extra set of photos for Merline to keep.

Walking Nancy into the apartment, Merline saw the place through the other woman's eyes, and she was quite proud of her home. She had picked out the cream-colored carpeting and the matching heavy linen drapes. She had searched the entire city for the perfect sofa and matching chair in dark brown velvet. The television was the latest floor model, and her kitchen was straight out of *Better Homes and Gardens*: shiny white appliances and sea green Formica cabinets. Kenny had chosen the art on the walls, colorful reproductions of abstract paintings.

After they were seated, Nancy took a packet of photos from her purse, and Merline noticed something else in her hand as well.

"I thought you might be interested in this," she said quietly, handing over a folded piece of newspaper. It was a wedding announcement.

Francis D. Whitman and Delia Dukes were married on December 23rd at city hall. The groom was the owner of Club Royale, a venerable Chicago jazz club that closed its doors in 1960. He is the son of the late Mr. and Mrs. Thomas J. Whitman, who founded the Whitman Chewing Gum empire fifty years ago. Mrs. Whitman is a club singer who got her start at Club Royale and has gone on to continue a successful singing career in the Chicago area. This is the first marriage for both.

Merline read the announcement twice before looking up at Nancy. She was filled with conflicting feelings: happiness, jealousy, regret. Nancy's eyes were understanding.

"This is your sister, right? I never knew her, but I knew of her, of course."

Merline didn't trust herself to speak.

"The announcement was posted in the *Chicago Tribune*. It was Katherine who noticed it, actually. She remembers meeting her aunt once when she was a small girl, but she had the name wrong. She called her . . ."

"Duck." Merline's voice was hoarse, and she cleared her throat before continuing. "We called her Duck."

Nancy's smile was uncertain. "Well, it seems no one calls her Duck anymore. We asked around, and she is quite well-known around Chicago. I mean, among those who like jazz music."

This last bit said what Nancy Banks thought about women who sang in jazz clubs for a living.

Merline felt suddenly defensive, protective in a way that was completely unfamiliar.

"She's done well for herself. I'm not surprised—she always was the smart one."

Nancy chose not to respond. She began to show Merline the photos of Katherine in her purple cap and gown. Merline dutifully admired the photos, but she couldn't stop thinking about Duck. She had left Texas, and it was probably the best thing that ever happened to her. Merline smiled to herself and let pride push aside all the other emotions battling for her attention. Delia Dukes Whitman. It was something to be proud of.

CHAPTER 15
"You've Really Got a Hold On Me"

Delia
Chicago, 1963

I married Francis Daniel Whitman on December 23, 1963. The wind was icy, but the sun shone high and bright in the sky, and I couldn't imagine a better day to become Delia Whitman. We drove to the courthouse in Francis's white Buick Rivera. I felt like a princess sitting in the passenger seat, the brown leather soft under my legs. I was especially in love with the state-of-the-art AM/FM radio, and I turned the knob to my favorite rhythm and blues station. Francis loved to listen to me sing when we were alone, and he smiled as I sang along to Sam Cooke's "You Send Me."

"You never sing jazz anymore," Francis said, raising his eyebrows. The Club Royale had been closed for three years, but Francis was a purist and didn't like a lot of the R&B coming out of Detroit.

I finished the song before answering. "Francis, times change. And I love soul music. I'm thinking about adding more to my act."

"Just don't leave jazz behind altogether. Your voice is tailor-made for jazz."

I sang a few bars of "At Last" and we grinned at each other, remembering that was my favorite song back when I first started working at the club.

"I would never forget my roots."

The traffic thickened, signaling we were close to city hall, and as we turned onto LaSalle, I drew in my breath. The building took up a square city block, and although I'd passed it or seen it in photos, I had never been inside the classic Greek revival-style building. It was imposing, a place where futures were decided. It was where my future would begin.

"It's so big," I said to Francis as we entered the building. He took my hand and smiled at me.

"Nervous?"

I nodded, swallowing over the lump in my throat. I was trying not to notice the people in the lobby looking at us as we walked toward the justice of the peace's office, still holding hands. It was legal for blacks and whites to marry in Illinois, but that didn't mean it was common. People were still reeling from President Kennedy's death in November, still talking about Martin Luther King's speech at the March on Washington in August. I imagined that the sight of my brown hand in Francis's white one was a reminder of how much the world was changing, and not everyone was excited about the changes.

And this was Chicago, not Greenville, where it was not only illegal but unthinkable. I thought about

Merline; I had been thinking about her a lot lately. I wondered how she was; I thought about her and Kenny and how things had gone so differently for them. But that had been puppy love, two kids making choices before they even understood who they were or what the world was like. I was a grown woman, thirty-three years old, and Francis was forty. We had chosen each other not out of secrecy and lust, but in friendship and trust.

A sudden aching took hold inside my chest. I wished I had family here to see me marrying the man I loved, to see me all grown up, to see the woman I had become. But too much time had passed, and I couldn't imagine calling Merline or Mother after all these years.

We stopped in front of the glass door to the judge's chambers. Francis squeezed my hand, then pulled me into his arms.

"Delia, I love you. I have never loved anyone the way I love you. And it has nothing to do with what the rest of the world thinks," he whispered, as if reading my thoughts. "Now, do you take this man to be your lawful, wedded husband?"

He kissed my cheek, his lips as light as a feather.

I smiled. "I do."

I sang at the Club Royale on the last night before Francis closed its doors for good in October 1960. It wasn't a big night—the crowd was thin and it was mid-week, not the best night for a jazz club under any circumstances. It wasn't my usual night, but Francis had insisted I be the last person to stand on the stage.

"Remember when you stood up here with a rag on your head, singing into a broom years ago?" he asked. "You wanted to sing so badly. It seems right to me that you be the last singer who ever sings at the Royale."

For months, there had been rumors that the club wasn't doing well. Francis wasn't booking the top acts anymore, and he couldn't compete with larger clubs like the Blue Note. The world was expanding, jazz was global, and rhythm and blues was the new pop music.

"You could book some of the Motown groups, change the focus of the club," I suggested months before the club went under. It was late, and we were sitting in his office. I talked while he went over the ledger and receipts, looking increasingly despondent.

I loved all the music coming out of Detroit, even more than I had loved the jazz standards. Negro singers and musicians were buzzing about Barry Gordy and the idea that the singles heard on the radio might be controlled by one of us. Usually, white producers routinely gave songs written by Negroes to white singers—without giving Negroes credit or money.

"Have you heard that guy Smokey Robinson sing? He's in the Miracles," I told Francis. I sang a verse and the chorus of "Shop Around."

Francis smiled, but his face was weary. "But jazz is what I love, Delia. It's why I opened this club. I think I'm too old to change."

I sat on the edge of my seat. "Come on, Francis. You're not old. Look around—everything is changing. Kennedy is going to be president!"

"Listen, I'm glad things are changing, but jazz is what I know. The music business might just have to go on without me and this club."

He looked so sad. I did the only thing I knew would cheer him up. I sang "A Tisket, a Tasket." Finally, he laughed.

"Okay, okay. Now, let me drive you home. It's late and you need your beauty sleep."

I feigned horror. "Why, Mr. Whitman, are you implying that I am not beautiful enough?"

This was a joke. I never thought of myself as beautiful. Even in the gowns I wore for gigs, even with my hair styled and my face made up, I still thought of myself as plain Duck.

Francis tilted his head and said, "No, Delia. I can't see how you could get much prettier than you are right now."

My cheeks grew warm, and as if he could see my discomfort, he busied himself helping me into my coat and ushering me out the door.

We were quiet in the car, but it was a companionable silence and neither of us felt the need to fill the car with nervous chitchat.

"How about we drive for a while? I love the city at this time of night."

"It's the night sky that makes it nice," I agreed. "The darkness is almost purple and the buildings look like magic."

Francis glanced over at me.

"You should have been a poet," he teased softly.

"I like to read and sing poetry. I leave the writing to others."

"Delia, I believe you could do anything you set your mind to. I'll bet you were a handful as a kid. As Duck."

We drove along the lake and I looked out at the water. It was a black as oil, and in the distance there was a pin-point of light, a solitary boat floating along. I thought about Greenville, Mother, Merline. I didn't really know what kind of child I had been, besides lonely.

"And now, you're a swan."

"I never liked that story. Even after the ugly duckling becomes a swan and everyone loves her, the original problem is still there."

He thought for a moment. "Everyone is still judging by the outside, by appearances."

I nodded. "I always wanted people to like me for me."

There was a long silence. Finally, he spoke.

"But you're beautiful on the inside and the outside. So being a swan isn't all bad."

He pulled to a stop outside my apartment. I didn't want the moment, the night, to end. He leaned closer to me.

"I mean it, Delia. I know this is coming out of the blue, and I don't blame you if you want to run into that apartment and pretend none of this ever happened. But I—"

I kissed him.

Later that night, in my bed, he finished his sentence.

"I love you, Delia."

Francis had waited as long as he could before closing the club, but by Halloween, the club was losing money every night. Although they had heard the rumors, the people who worked behind the scenes were devastated by the loss of their jobs. It wasn't just the work that mattered; it was also the fact that most people, myself included, appreciated the difference between having a boss like Francis and a boss who didn't care about his employees. The kind of steady work the Club Royale provided was rare.

After singing that last night, I returned the next day to collect my things from the dressing room, which was down the hall from the employees' locker room and lounge. Rose no longer worked at the club, but I still knew most of the others from when we had worked together. After I moved from maid to singer, they were pleasant, but none of them had much to say to me, which was not so different from how things had been before.

But that morning when I stopped in to say goodbye, I sensed a dark hostility that made the chilled air inside the room feel even colder. Until that moment, I hadn't thought much about what I had left behind when I stepped onto the stage. When I was cleaning the club, life wasn't good, but it was simple and familiar. I was in escape mode, thinking about my life in terms of *not* being in Greenville. I hadn't given much thought to what would come next. And then came Marv—and Francis—and my future was decided.

I now felt silly for not realizing that others might see my singing career as unfair. No one except Francis knew what Marvin had done to me, and so they didn't understand the price I had paid for my "good fortune."

Even so, I felt guilty standing there in my expensive shoes and tailored coat.

"I'm going to miss this place," I said. "I mopped those floors enough times to know every fleck and chip by heart."

There were ten people in the room, but only one man looked up at me when I spoke.

Donald Richmond had been one of the first people I met when I came to Chicago. He was the one who showed me around the club when I answered the ad for a job. About a month later, he asked me out to dinner. Donald had skin like black coffee and a voice that was deep and smooth. When we met, I thought that he must be a singer, because his baritone was unlike any other I'd heard. When he smiled at me, my stomach fluttered. I had never had a crush on anyone and, for the first time, I had an inkling of what Merline and Kenny had shared back home in Texas.

It was summer, and I couldn't believe how hot it was. When I imagined Chicago, I had always thought of the cold, the wind, and those first winters lived up to my expectations. But before I experienced my first Chicago winter, there was the sluggish humidity of a Midwestern summer. Despite the heat, people did not slow their pace. Everyone was in a rush, sweeping by me on the sidewalks, giving me annoyed glances when I waited for the walk signals at corners. It wasn't just that people walked fast, either. They also spoke quickly, and sometimes I had to ask strangers to repeat directions because I couldn't decipher the rapid sound of their nasal voices. I also got used to repeating my own words, discovering that I, too, had an accent.

Donald pointed this out to me as he showed me around the club.

"I like the way you talk," he told me. "It reminds me of back home. But people up here will give you a hard time about having an accent."

"What accent?"

I must have looked genuinely perplexed because Donald grinned. My cheeks burned with embarrassment, but Donald's smile was gentle, not mocking.

"You can't hear how you sound different from everyone around here?"

I had assumed the differences were about speed, but when I thought about it, he was right, it was about more than speech patterns. People in Chicago called soda *pop*, and they sounded as if their sinuses were blocked when they said *Wis-cahn-sin*.

"I've never lived anywhere except Greenville, and everyone there sounds like me," I said.

After walking through the entire club, we returned to the main room. I looked at the stage and wondered what it would feel like to be up there.

"So, you want the job? It's a good place to work."

What I wanted was to stand on stage and sing, but I was too practical to say it aloud.

"I want the job."

Donald smiled his approval. "We could use more pretty girls around here. Lightens up the place."

That was the first time I felt the flutter.

And that scared me. I was all alone, seventeen years old and in a strange new city. I didn't know who or what I would end up being, but I knew for sure I didn't want to end up like Merline. I didn't know much about men, sex, and love, but the little I knew scared me. When I looked at Donald, I was scared of how he made me feel.

So I said no to dinner, making up some excuse. He kept asking and I kept refusing until he gave up. But he had remained friendly to me until I started singing. And when the club closed eight years later, he stood looking at me with disgust in his eyes.

"Oh, you'll miss it? Miss what, being on stage, showing off?"

I swallowed hard. "I'll miss it all," I said quietly.

"So while the rest of us are trying to find jobs, trying to feed our families, trying to survive, you'll be sitting around being all nostalgic." His tone was sharp, and someone sitting on the other side of the room snickered.

I didn't know what to say, but it didn't matter. Donald never gave me the chance to defend myself.

"Oh, that's right. You're close with Mister Whitman, right? So we know at least one person who will be okay." Donald made his voice syrupy sweet, but he spat out Francis's name with venom.

"What do you mean?" I felt queasy, because I knew exactly what he meant. He thought that I'd slept my way onto the stage, that back in 1952 I had given my body to Francis Whitman in exchange for a career.

Donald had the details wrong, though. I wanted to tell him and the others how Marvin Whitman had raped me, how he'd changed me forever. He had taken what he wanted and everything changed for me that night. I wanted to tell Donald how Francis had been there, at my bedside in the hospital even as he grieved for his brother. I wanted them all to understand that I had paid a price, yes, but it wasn't to Francis.

Most of all, I wanted to explain that I finally thought I understood love. It came when it wanted, without reason or logic. Francis was the man I loved, and it didn't matter whether he was white or how we'd found each other. It was just love.

"You're wrong about me," I whispered, wiping tears away. Donald just rolled his eyes and turned away.

"White man's whore," someone hissed as I left the room.

I paused briefly, and then I stood up straighter and continued out the door.

I found it hard to focus on the words of the wedding ceremony. Repeating the traditional vows and exchanging rings felt beside the point. What Francis and I had wasn't about rituals and symbols. What we had was about us. I watched Francis when it was his turn to speak. His hair was longer in the back than it had been when we met in 1947. The crinkles around his eyes stayed put whether he was laughing or not. Even though we weren't having a formal wedding, he had worn his tuxedo, and his shoes shone like mirrors. Francis was a good man, a compassionate man, and although tragedy had brought us together, friendship was what kept us together.

"I now pronounce you man and wife. You may kiss the bride."

Francis hugged me first, then gently pressed his lips against mine. And I became Delia Dukes Whitman.

CHAPTER 16
"Call Me"

Merline
Dallas, 1970

It wasn't until Violet died that Merline learned that "ashes to ashes, dust to dust" isn't actually in the King James Bible. It's a part of the Book of Common Prayer, and Merline knew Mother would want the Book of Common Prayer quoted at her funeral. Her mother was old-fashioned, a firm believer in the King James Bible, even though Merline had never known her to go to church and she had scoffed whenever religion was mentioned.

The task of finding a reading for Violet's funeral fell to Merline by default. They hadn't seen Duck since the day she left Greenville when she was seventeen years old. Rollins had died of a massive heart attack two years ago. Katherine was now a white woman, married to a white man, her transition into the white world now complete. There was no one else to organize the funeral, and for all the years of silence between them, Merline knew it was right to do this one last thing for her mother. No sense in holding grudges against the dead.

Merline had seen Violet a lot in the weeks before she died. Her mother had been sick for a long time and had never bothered to go to the doctor. By the time she collapsed while grocery shopping, cancer had spread through her body and she had only weeks to live.

It must have taken a lot for Violet to call Merline. They hadn't spoken since the day she'd kicked her—seventeen and pregnant with Kenny's child—out of the house. Merline had been too proud to ever try to contact her mother, and she assumed that the same coldness that allowed Violet to put her daughter out into the street was what kept her from making contact over the years. Greenville was a small town, so there was no question that Violet could have found Merline if she wanted to. Twenty-eight years had passed, and they had not spoken one word to each other until a month before Violet died.

"You're the only one I can count on to come see me," Violet croaked one evening as Merline sat by her bed.

Merline considered this. Who else did her mother think was left to come visit her? She remembered what the doctors said about the tumors in her mother's brain. They had warned that she might not be coherent. Merline had been leaving work early to spend afternoons and evenings with her, and, most of the time, they sat silently, her mother floating in and out of consciousness, high on morphine and low on time.

"Duck would come if she knew. Did you call her?"

Violet shook her head and waved a hand in the air, as if to say that Duck wasn't worth the effort. Though bothered by her mother's response, Merline still couldn't bring herself to ask why she had never seemed to love Duck. And she wanted to know why Violet had been unable to love her enough to help her when she most needed her family. But what was the point, now?

She had considered calling her sister, but thought better of it when she recalled the wedding announcement from back in 1963. She decided that Duck was better off staying away. Her sister had found someone to spend her life with, and Merline hoped she was happy, needed to believe that her little sister was happy. The older she became, the more she thought about Duck, now Delia, in Chicago. She still liked to go on walks, but now, she walked in Dallas parks and dreamed not of her own fantasy lives, but of Duck's. She imagined the details—about Duck's husband, about her singing, about the furs she wore to guard against cold winter days. In her fantasies, her sister never had children. Her experience with her own child had been disappointing on the best days and heartbreaking on the worst. No, she hoped Delia Whitman had a romantic, simple, carefree life. She hoped that she had more in her life than another woman's husband, a boring job, and a neat but lonely apartment in the city.

On Violet's better days, she was able to sit up in bed and talk in a hoarse voice, though Merline couldn't understand some of what her mother said. She didn't recognize the names she muttered: Phoebe, Rose, Holloway. She knew the name Grayson—her father—but she didn't know anything about him except he died when she was just a baby. When Violet said something about "Grayson and his damned politics," Merline sat forward in her chair, anxious to hear more. But Violet grew silent and gazed out the window at the summer sun, still bright in the sky, though it was nearly seven o'clock in the evening. It was mid-June, and Merline didn't think her mother would make it to Independence Day.

Merline was comfortable with silence. After a long while, Violet started coughing, coughing, coughing as if she might never stop. Merline reached out and handed her a cup of water.

"I need to say something."

"We can talk later. It's getting late."

"No, now, I want to say this now. I was wrong."

She paused to take a sip of water.

"All those years, I thought that if I kept you at arm's length, it would be easier for me. If I didn't love you, then it wouldn't hurt when I lost you. But I loved you, anyway, you and Duck, and when I lost you, it was just like it was every other time, except worse because you were my babies."

Merline sat still, watching her mother cry. She had never seen her mother cry, had never even imagined that the woman was capable of this kind of emotion. It was a surreal moment for her, a forty-five-year-old woman watching her sixty-one-year-old dying mother sobbing.

She didn't know what to say or what do to. Each sob made Merline wince, made her more uncomfortable. She did not cry, would not cry, not now. As Violet's tears ran their course, she grew quiet.

"You can't help who you love. I learned that a long time ago," Merline said quietly.

Violet soon fell asleep and Merline watched her for a long time before she finally headed back to her apartment. It was a long drive, but she wouldn't even consider staying the night in her childhood home. She knew better than to visit the ghosts of her innocence, even after all these years.

Violet died the next day.

CHAPTER 17
"The Long and Winding Road"

Delia
Chicago, 1970

After seven hours of labor, three weeks of bed rest, and years of thinking I couldn't have children, Dawn was born. Many mothers were still being knocked out for births, but I wanted a natural birth. I was forty years old, and Francis and I had spent nine months laughing in wonder at this late pregnancy that took us both by surprise.

We wanted children from the moment we married, but after a few years, the doctors told us it wasn't going to happen. So we mourned for a while, then we went about the business of making a life for just the two of us. Francis spent his days investing in music studios and production companies. I spent my days giving voice lessons and my nights happily at home with Francis. It was a simple life, one that we both appreciated.

And then, during the fall of 1969, I started to feel queasy and tired all the time, and no matter what I did, I never felt any better. I was three months along before either of us considered that I might be pregnant. It was my doctor who suggested the pregnancy test, just to cover all the bases. I'll never forget the dumbfounded look on Francis's face when I told him that he was going to be a father.

"I hope it's a boy," I said one night. By my seventh month, my belly was an enormous lump and the tiny baby kicking inside me kept me from sleeping. Francis lay beside me through most nights, talking to me, making me laugh, taking my mind off the discomfort. We spent those long nights in the dim light of one small lamp, imagining who our child would be.

"He'll be tall and serious, like you," I said. "He'll grow up to be a senator."

Francis shook his head. "I would like a daughter. Someone sweet and strong, like you," he said. "She could still be a senator."

Some nights, Francis couldn't help falling asleep, and I thought about my mother and Merline. I didn't know anything about babies, and I didn't know anything about being a mother. Would I be like my own mother, cold and detached? Was that kind of thing genetic?

I wondered about Merline and Katherine. What were their lives like? Katherine was a grown woman. Were they still in Texas? What would Mother and Merline think of Delia? Duck now seemed like a person separate from my true self, a part of a distant past that no longer mattered to me. Being pregnant made me think of family, and it was the first time I ever seriously considered finding mine.

I didn't tell Francis about these thoughts. He still got upset whenever I mentioned my mother, the way she had chosen Rollins over me. I knew he wouldn't want me to call, to risk another type of rejection. He protected me as he always had, and I loved him for it.

Dawn was born a week early, as if she couldn't wait to discover the world. My doctor had given us warnings about older mothers and birth defects, so when Dawn was born, I made sure to look her over carefully so I could spot anything wrong. But she was a perfect six-pound baby with a head full of straight black hair. She let out a squawk that the nurses said was louder than any baby they'd ever heard, and when they lay her on my chest, I laughed at the red fury on her face. She was a fighter. I fell in love that very moment, and I never again doubted that I could be a good mother to her.

I handed my screaming bundle to Francis. He took her gingerly, as if he was afraid to touch her. He held her slightly away from his chest, like a fragile piece of blown glass. He looked worried, and, for just a moment, I thought he'd seen something that I had missed.

Before I could say anything, one of the nurses stepped closer.

"Don't worry, Mr. Whitman. Holding her close won't hurt her. She's tough."

Francis drew Dawn in closer to his body, and her crying stopped. A grin spread over his face, and he looked at me.

"Just like her mother," he said.

The next day, Francis went home to shower and change, and he took the call. It was Merline telling us Violet had died.

CHAPTER 18

"Ain't No Mountain High Enough"

Delia and Merline
Greenville, Summer 1970

Violet Dukes Rollins was buried in Restful Gardens cemetery on July 1, 1970. It was an oasis of green lawn and mature trees that shaded graves large and small. Its layout had no obvious design. It was one of the older burial grounds in Texas, and until recently only blacks were buried there. Large headstones with elaborate inscriptions stood next to modest markers that simply listed names and dates. The sites were all swept free of leaves, either by conscientious family members or sympathetic groundskeepers, many of whom had relatives buried in the cemetery. It was a tradition for blacks to honor the dead by keeping the final resting places in good condition. Greenville blacks were raised never to speak ill of those who have passed on, and to make sure that no matter how deep the rifts between family members, one must respect the dead. Restful Gardens reflected that tradition, and Violet's marker was the best available. Merline made sure Kenny paid for the funeral expenses and the tombstone for the mother from whom she'd been estranged most of her life.

The group gathered around Violet's gravesite was mismatched and varied, like a human mosaic. Delia held baby Dawn in her arms and stood next to Francis, who held a black umbrella over them. She was already able to fit back into a black dress, though Dawn was born just a week before, and she wore high heels that threatened to sink into the muddy grass. Oversized black sunglasses covered her eyes and caught the tears that pooled at the bottom of the frames. She couldn't decide why she was crying. She hadn't seen Violet in nearly twenty-five years, and when she lived with her mother, the woman had treated her more like an unwanted burden than a daughter. She looked over at Merline, who wore a stylish linen suit and no sunglasses. There were no tears to hide on her face, just a serious but calm look, as if she were attending the funeral of a distant acquaintance rather than her mother.

It was steaming hot already, though it was barely nine o'clock in the morning, and it had been raining for hours. Delia shivered and looked down to make sure Dawn was still asleep. She drew closer to Francis, who was formal and serious in his dark suit, his shirt starched and seemingly unaffected by the rain that dripped from the edges of the umbrella onto his sleeves.

Merline stood across from Delia, watching her, trying to find her little sister Duck in this self-possessed woman. They made a perfect threesome: Delia, her husband, and the baby she had been surprised to hear of when she'd called about Violet. Surely, her sister was too old to have a baby? Merline looked at the baby for a long time. A little girl, with buttery skin and dark hair. Glancing over at Katherine, now twenty-seven years old, she said a silent prayer that the girl would darken as she grew older.

Katherine was in a group with Nancy Banks, who sat in a wheelchair and sometimes seemed uncertain of where she was and why. Kenny stood behind his mother, his hands resting lightly on the handles of her chair. Priscilla stood next to him, clinging to his sleeve and glaring at Merline whenever their eyes met. Kenny noticed and gave Merline an apologetic smile when Priscilla wasn't looking, but Merline looked away. Next to Katherine stood her husband, a pale red-haired man named Sonny. He was a soldier and would be on his way to Vietnam in a few weeks. Katherine and Sonny had come back to Greenville to help care for Nancy, whose health was steadily fading. They lived in the Banks home, that big old house where Katherine had spent her early years. Merline refused to go back to that house, and she had seen little of Katherine since she moved back home.

Delia tried to listen to the prayer being recited by the reverend, but she couldn't stop looking at the person she assumed was Katherine, standing not with Merline but with Kenny's mother. Had she seen her anywhere else, she would have assumed she was a typical white woman: long blonde hair, fair skin. Delia saw the way her sister looked at Katherine, and she knew that this must be the baby that had changed everything for Merline.

The minister, a dark-skinned man none of them knew because none of them had been to church in many years, read from Psalm 32. Violet had made this request, and Merline made sure that her mother had her final wish granted. The reverend had suggested reading just a part of Psalm 32, but Merline insisted that Violet wanted *all* of it read, not just verses one through five, as he preferred.

Nevertheless, he read the passage with emotion, and by the end of his reading, each person among the small group clustered around the grave stood still, their thoughts not of each other, but of Violet.

Psalm 32: The Joy of Forgiveness
Blessed is he whose transgression is forgiven, whose sin is covered.

Blessed is the man unto whom the LORD imputeth not iniquity, and in whose spirit there is no guile.

When I kept silence, my bones waxed old through my roaring all the day long.

For day and night thy hand was heavy upon me: my moisture is turned into the drought of summer.

I acknowledge my sin unto thee, and mine iniquity have I not hid. I said, I will confess my transgressions unto the LORD; and thou forgavest the iniquity of my sin.

For this shall every one that is godly pray unto thee in a time when thou mayest be found: surely in the floods of great waters they shall not come nigh unto him.

Thou art my hiding place; thou shalt preserve me from trouble; thou shalt compass me about with songs of deliverance.

I will instruct thee and teach thee in the way which thou shalt go: I will guide thee with mine eye.

Be ye not as the horse, or as the mule, which have no understanding: whose mouth must be held in with bit and bridle, lest they come near unto thee.

Many sorrows shall be to the wicked: but he that trusteth in the LORD, mercy shall compass him about.

Be glad in the LORD, and rejoice, ye righteous: and shout for joy, all ye that are upright in heart.

And with that, Violet Dukes was laid to rest. As they walked away, her daughters thought about the words. Both had been the object of Violet's sin. They had suffered many sorrows, but neither believed she was wicked. Glancing around, they thought of the many times she had kept silent. As they walked slowly through the muddied grass, their eyes met for a moment.

Delia smiled at Merline. Merline, after a moment, smiled back. She slowed her steps to fall in next to Delia.

They strolled together for a while, until the rest of the group was well ahead of them. The rain had slowed to a fine mist, and Delia took off her sunglasses and stopped underneath the canopy of an old oak tree. She adjusted Dawn's blanket and held her daughter's head to her face, taking in the sweet baby smell.

"Can I hold her?"

Delia nodded and handed Dawn to Merline, who held her expertly, as if her own days as a new mother were fresh in her memory.

"She's beautiful."

Delia smiled. "I think she looks like Francis."

Merline shook her head, examining the baby carefully. "No, I think she looks like you."

She held out her free hand, and Delia clasped it. Together, they turned and walked away.

The End

2010 Mass Market Titles

January

Show Me The Sun
Miriam Shumba
ISBN: 978-158571-405-6
$6.99

Promises of Forever
Celya Bowers
ISBN: 978-1-58571-380-6
$6.99

February

Love Out Of Order
Nicole Green
ISBN: 978-1-58571-381-3
$6.99

Unclear and Present Danger
Michele Cameron
ISBN: 978-158571-408-7
$6.99

March

Stolen Jewels
Michele Sudler
ISBN: 978-158571-409-4
$6.99

Not Quite Right
Tammy Williams
ISBN: 978-158571-410-0
$6.99

April

Oak Bluffs
Joan Early
ISBN: 978-1-58571-379-0
$6.99

Crossing The Line
Bernice Layton
ISBN: 978-158571-412-4
$6.99

How To Kill Your Husband
Keith Walker
ISBN: 978-158571-421-6
$6.99

May

The Business of Love
Cheris F. Hodges
ISBN: 978-158571-373-8
$6.99

Wayward Dreams
Gail McFarland
ISBN: 978-158571-422-3
$6.99

June

The Doctor's Wife
Mildred Riley
ISBN: 978-158571-424-7
$6.99

Mixed Reality
Chamein Canton
ISBN: 978-158571-423-0
$6.99

2010 Mass Market Titles (continued)

July

Blue Interlude
Keisha Mennefee
ISBN: 978-158571-378-3
$6.99

Always You
Crystal Hubbard
ISBN: 978-158571-371-4
$6.99

Unbeweavable
Katrina Spencer
ISBN: 978-158571-426-1
$6.99

August

Small Sensations
Crystal V. Rhodes
ISBN: 978-158571-376-9
$6.99

Let's Get It On
Dyanne Davis
ISBN: 978-158571-416-2
$6.99

September

Unconditional
A.C. Arthur
ISBN: 978-158571-413-1
$6.99

Swan
Africa Fine
ISBN: 978-158571-377-6
$6.99$6.99

October

Friends in Need
Joan Early
ISBN:978-1-58571-428-5
$6.99

Against the Wind
Gwynne Forster
ISBN:978-158571-429-2
$6.99

That Which Has Horns
Miriam Shumba
ISBN:978-1-58571-430-8
$6.99

November

A Good Dude
Keith Walker
ISBN:978-1-58571-431-5
$6.99

Reye's Gold
Ruthie Robinson
ISBN:978-1-58571-432-2
$6.99

December

Still Waters...
Crystal V. Rhodes
ISBN:978-1-58571-433-9
$6.99

Burn
Crystal Hubbard
ISBN: 978-1-58571-406-3
$6.99

Other Genesis Press, Inc. Titles

2 Good	Celya Bowers	$6.99
A Dangerous Deception	J.M. Jeffries	$8.95
A Dangerous Love	J.M. Jeffries	$8.95
A Dangerous Obsession	J.M. Jeffries	$8.95
A Drummer's Beat to Mend	Kei Swanson	$9.95
A Happy Life	Charlotte Harris	$9.95
A Heart's Awakening	Veronica Parker	$9.95
A Lark on the Wing	Phyliss Hamilton	$9.95
A Love of Her Own	Cheris F. Hodges	$9.95
A Love to Cherish	Beverly Clark	$8.95
A Place Like Home	Alicia Wiggins	$6.99
A Risk of Rain	Dar Tomlinson	$8.95
A Taste of Temptation	Reneé Alexis	$9.95
A Twist of Fate	Beverly Clark	$8.95
A Voice Behind Thunder	Carrie Elizabeth Greene	$6.99
A Will to Love	Angie Daniels	$9.95
Acquisitions	Kimberley White	$8.95
Across	Carol Payne	$12.95
After the Vows	Leslie Esdaile	$10.95
(Summer Anthology)	T.T. Henderson	
	Jacqueline Thomas	
Again, My Love	Kayla Perrin	$10.95
Against the Wind	Gwynne Forster	$8.95
All I Ask	Barbara Keaton	$8.95
All I'll Ever Need	Mildred Riley	$6.99
Always You	Crystal Hubbard	$6.99
Ambrosia	T.T. Henderson	$8.95
An Unfinished Love Affair	Barbara Keaton	$8.95
And Then Came You	Dorothy Elizabeth Love	$8.95
Angel's Paradise	Janice Angelique	$9.95
Another Memory	Pamela Ridley	$6.99
Anything But Love	Celya Bowers	$6.99
At Last	Lisa G. Riley	$8.95
Best Foot Forward	Michele Sudler	$6.99
Best of Friends	Natalie Dunbar	$8.95
Best of Luck Elsewhere	Trisha Haddad	$6.99
Beyond the Rapture	Beverly Clark	$9.95
Blame It on Paradise	Crystal Hubbard	$6.99
Blaze	Barbara Keaton	$9.95
Blindsided	Tammy Williams	$6.99
Bliss, Inc.	Chamein Canton	$6.99
Blood Lust	J.M.Jeffries	$9.95

Other Genesis Press, Inc. Titles (continued)

Blood Seduction	J.M. Jeffries	$9.95
Bodyguard	Andrea Jackson	$9.95
Boss of Me	Diana Nyad	$8.95
Bound by Love	Beverly Clark	$8.95
Breeze	Robin Hampton Allen	$10.95
Broken	Dar Tomlinson	$24.95
By Design	Barbara Keaton	$8.95
Cajun Heat	Charlene Berry	$8.95
Careless Whispers	Rochelle Alers	$8.95
Cats & Other Tales	Marilyn Wagner	$8.95
Caught in a Trap	Andre Michelle	$8.95
Caught Up in the Rapture	Lisa G. Riley	$9.95
Cautious Heart	Cheris F. Hodges	$8.95
Chances	Pamela Leigh Starr	$8.95
Checks and Balances	Elaine Sims	$6.99
Cherish the Flame	Beverly Clark	$8.95
Choices	Tammy Williams	$6.99
Class Reunion	Irma Jenkins/ John Brown	$12.95
Code Name: Diva	J.M. Jeffries	$9.95
Conquering Dr. Wexler's Heart	Kimberley White	$9.95
Corporate Seduction	A.C. Arthur	$9.95
Crossing Paths, Tempting Memories	Dorothy Elizabeth Love	$9.95
Crush	Crystal Hubbard	$9.95
Cypress Whisperings	Phyllis Hamilton	$8.95
Dark Embrace	Crystal Wilson Harris	$8.95
Dark Storm Rising	Chinelu Moore	$10.95
Daughter of the Wind	Joan Xian	$8.95
Dawn's Harbor	Kymberly Hunt	$6.99
Deadly Sacrifice	Jack Kean	$22.95
Designer Passion	Dar Tomlinson Diana Richeaux	$8.95
Do Over	Celya Bowers	$9.95
Dream Keeper	Gail McFarland	$6.99
Dream Runner	Gail McFarland	$6.99
Dreamtective	Liz Swados	$5.95
Ebony Angel	Deatri King-Bey	$9.95
Ebony Butterfly II	Delilah Dawson	$14.95
Echoes of Yesterday	Beverly Clark	$9.95
Eden's Garden	Elizabeth Rose	$8.95

Other Genesis Press, Inc. Titles (continued)

Eve's Prescription	Edwina Martin Arnold	$8.95
Everlastin' Love	Gay G. Gunn	$8.95
Everlasting Moments	Dorothy Elizabeth Love	$8.95
Everything and More	Sinclair Lebeau	$8.95
Everything But Love	Natalie Dunbar	$8.95
Falling	Natalie Dunbar	$9.95
Fate	Pamela Leigh Starr	$8.95
Finding Isabella	A.J. Garrotto	$8.95
Fireflies	Joan Early	$6.99
Fixin' Tyrone	Keith Walker	$6.99
Forbidden Quest	Dar Tomlinson	$10.95
Forever Love	Wanda Y. Thomas	$8.95
From the Ashes	Kathleen Suzanne Jeanne Sumerix	$8.95
Frost On My Window	Angela Weaver	$6.99
Gentle Yearning	Rochelle Alers	$10.95
Glory of Love	Sinclair LeBeau	$10.95
Go Gentle Into That Good Night	Malcom Boyd	$12.95
Goldengroove	Mary Beth Craft	$16.95
Groove, Bang, and Jive	Steve Cannon	$8.99
Hand in Glove	Andrea Jackson	$9.95
Hard to Love	Kimberley White	$9.95
Hart & Soul	Angie Daniels	$8.95
Heart of the Phoenix	A.C. Arthur	$9.95
Heartbeat	Stephanie Bedwell-Grime	$8.95
Hearts Remember	M. Loui Quezada	$8.95
Hidden Memories	Robin Allen	$10.95
Higher Ground	Leah Latimer	$19.95
Hitler, the War, and the Pope	Ronald Rychiak	$26.95
How to Write a Romance	Kathryn Falk	$18.95
I Married a Reclining Chair	Lisa M. Fuhs	$8.95
I'll Be Your Shelter	Giselle Carmichael	$8.95
I'll Paint a Sun	A.J. Garrotto	$9.95
Icie	Pamela Leigh Starr	$8.95
If I Were Your Woman	LaConnie Taylor-Jones	$6.99
Illusions	Pamela Leigh Starr	$8.95
Indigo After Dark Vol. I	Nia Dixon/Angelique	$10.95
Indigo After Dark Vol. II	Dolores Bundy/ Cole Riley	$10.95
Indigo After Dark Vol. III	Montana Blue/ Coco Morena	$10.95

Other Genesis Press, Inc. Titles (continued)

Indigo After Dark Vol. IV	Cassandra Colt/	$14.95
Indigo After Dark Vol. V	Delilah Dawson	$14.95
Indiscretions	Donna Hill	$8.95
Intentional Mistakes	Michele Sudler	$9.95
Interlude	Donna Hill	$8.95
Intimate Intentions	Angie Daniels	$8.95
It's in the Rhythm	Sammie Ward	$6.99
It's Not Over Yet	J.J. Michael	$9.95
Jolie's Surrender	Edwina Martin-Arnold	$8.95
Kiss or Keep	Debra Phillips	$8.95
Lace	Giselle Carmichael	$9.95
Lady Preacher	K.T. Richey	$6.99
Last Train to Memphis	Elsa Cook	$12.95
Lasting Valor	Ken Olsen	$24.95
Let Us Prey	Hunter Lundy	$25.95
Lies Too Long	Pamela Ridley	$13.95
Life Is Never As It Seems	J.J. Michael	$12.95
Lighter Shade of Brown	Vicki Andrews	$8.95
Look Both Ways	Joan Early	$6.99
Looking for Lily	Africa Fine	$6.99
Love Always	Mildred E. Riley	$10.95
Love Doesn't Come Easy	Charlyne Dickerson	$8.95
Love Unveiled	Gloria Greene	$10.95
Love's Deception	Charlene Berry	$10.95
Love's Destiny	M. Loui Quezada	$8.95
Love's Secrets	Yolanda McVey	$6.99
Mae's Promise	Melody Walcott	$8.95
Magnolia Sunset	Giselle Carmichael	$8.95
Many Shades of Gray	Dyanne Davis	$6.99
Matters of Life and Death	Lesego Malepe, Ph.D.	$15.95
Meant to Be	Jeanne Sumerix	$8.95
Midnight Clear	Leslie Esdaile	$10.95
(Anthology)	Gwynne Forster	
	Carmen Green	
	Monica Jackson	
Midnight Magic	Gwynne Forster	$8.95
Midnight Peril	Vicki Andrews	$10.95
Misconceptions	Pamela Leigh Starr	$9.95
Moments of Clarity	Michele Cameron	$6.99
Montgomery's Children	Richard Perry	$14.95
Mr. Fix-It	Crystal Hubbard	$6.99
My Buffalo Soldier	Barbara B.K. Reeves	$8.95

Other Genesis Press, Inc. Titles (continued)

Naked Soul	Gwynne Forster	$8.95
Never Say Never	Michele Cameron	$6.99
Next to Last Chance	Louisa Dixon	$24.95
No Apologies	Seressia Glass	$8.95
No Commitment Required	Seressia Glass	$8.95
No Regrets	Mildred E. Riley	$8.95
Not His Type	Chamein Canton	$6.99
Nowhere to Run	Gay G. Gunn	$10.95
O Bed! O Breakfast!	Rob Kuehnle	$14.95
Object of His Desire	A.C. Arthur	$8.95
Office Policy	A.C. Arthur	$9.95
Once in a Blue Moon	Dorianne Cole	$9.95
One Day at a Time	Bella McFarland	$8.95
One of These Days	Michele Sudler	$9.95
Outside Chance	Louisa Dixon	$24.95
Passion	T.T. Henderson	$10.95
Passion's Blood	Cherif Fortin	$22.95
Passion's Furies	AlTonya Washington	$6.99
Passion's Journey	Wanda Y. Thomas	$8.95
Past Promises	Jahmel West	$8.95
Path of Fire	T.T. Henderson	$8.95
Path of Thorns	Annetta P. Lee	$9.95
Peace Be Still	Colette Haywood	$12.95
Picture Perfect	Reon Carter	$8.95
Playing for Keeps	Stephanie Salinas	$8.95
Pride & Joi	Gay G. Gunn	$8.95
Promises Made	Bernice Layton	$6.99
Promises to Keep	Alicia Wiggins	$8.95
Quiet Storm	Donna Hill	$10.95
Reckless Surrender	Rochelle Alers	$6.95
Red Polka Dot in a World Full of Plaid	Varian Johnson	$12.95
Red Sky	Renee Alexis	$6.99
Reluctant Captive	Joyce Jackson	$8.95
Rendezvous With Fate	Jeanne Sumerix	$8.95
Revelations	Cheris F. Hodges	$8.95
Rivers of the Soul	Leslie Esdaile	$8.95
Rocky Mountain Romance	Kathleen Suzanne	$8.95
Rooms of the Heart	Donna Hill	$8.95
Rough on Rats and Tough on Cats	Chris Parker	$12.95
Save Me	Africa Fine	$6.99

Other Genesis Press, Inc. Titles (continued)

Secret Library Vol. 1	Nina Sheridan	$18.95
Secret Library Vol. 2	Cassandra Colt	$8.95
Secret Thunder	Annetta P. Lee	$9.95
Shades of Brown	Denise Becker	$8.95
Shades of Desire	Monica White	$8.95
Shadows in the Moonlight	Jeanne Sumerix	$8.95
Sin	Crystal Rhodes	$8.95
Singing A Song...	Crystal Rhodes	$6.99
Six O'Clock	Katrina Spencer	$6.99
Small Whispers	Annetta P. Lee	$6.99
So Amazing	Sinclair LeBeau	$8.95
Somebody's Someone	Sinclair LeBeau	$8.95
Someone to Love	Alicia Wiggins	$8.95
Song in the Park	Martin Brant	$15.95
Soul Eyes	Wayne L. Wilson	$12.95
Soul to Soul	Donna Hill	$8.95
Southern Comfort	J.M. Jeffries	$8.95
Southern Fried Standards	S.R. Maddox	$6.99
Still the Storm	Sharon Robinson	$8.95
Still Waters Run Deep	Leslie Esdaile	$8.95
Stolen Memories	Michele Sudler	$6.99
Stories to Excite You	Anna Forrest/Divine	$14.95
Storm	Pamela Leigh Starr	$6.99
Subtle Secrets	Wanda Y. Thomas	$8.95
Suddenly You	Crystal Hubbard	$9.95
Sweet Repercussions	Kimberley White	$9.95
Sweet Sensations	Gwyneth Bolton	$9.95
Sweet Tomorrows	Kimberly White	$8.95
Taken by You	Dorothy Elizabeth Love	$9.95
Tattooed Tears	T. T. Henderson	$8.95
Tempting Faith	Crystal Hubbard	$6.99
The Color Line	Lizzette Grayson Carter	$9.95
The Color of Trouble	Dyanne Davis	$8.95
The Disappearance of	Kayla Perrin	$5.95
Allison Jones		
The Fires Within	Beverly Clark	$9.95
The Foursome	Celya Bowers	$6.99
The Honey Dipper's Legacy	Myra Pannell-Allen	$14.95
The Joker's Love Tune	Sidney Rickman	$15.95
The Little Pretender	Barbara Cartland	$10.95
The Love We Had	Natalie Dunbar	$8.95
The Man Who Could Fly	Bob & Milana Beamon	$18.95

Other Genesis Press, Inc. Titles (continued)

The Missing Link	Charlyne Dickerson	$8.95
The Mission	Pamela Leigh Starr	$6.99
The More Things Change	Chamein Canton	$6.99
The Perfect Frame	Beverly Clark	$9.95
The Price of Love	Sinclair LeBeau	$8.95
The Smoking Life	Ilene Barth	$29.95
The Words of the Pitcher	Kei Swanson	$8.95
Things Forbidden	Maryam Diaab	$6.99
This Life Isn't Perfect Holla	Sandra Foy	$6.99
Three Doors Down	Michele Sudler	$6.99
Three Wishes	Seressia Glass	$8.95
Ties That Bind	Kathleen Suzanne	$8.95
Tiger Woods	Libby Hughes	$5.95
Time Is of the Essence	Angie Daniels	$9.95
Timeless Devotion	Bella McFarland	$9.95
Tomorrow's Promise	Leslie Esdaile	$8.95
Truly Inseparable	Wanda Y. Thomas	$8.95
Two Sides to Every Story	Dyanne Davis	$9.95
Unbreak My Heart	Dar Tomlinson	$8.95
Uncommon Prayer	Kenneth Swanson	$9.95
Unconditional Love	Alicia Wiggins	$8.95
Unconditional	A.C. Arthur	$9.95
Undying Love	Renee Alexis	$6.99
Until Death Do Us Part	Susan Paul	$8.95
Vows of Passion	Bella McFarland	$9.95
Waiting for Mr. Darcy	Chamein Canton	$6.99
Waiting in the Shadows	Michele Sudler	$6.99
Wedding Gown	Dyanne Davis	$8.95
What's Under Benjamin's Bed	Sandra Schaffer	$8.95
When a Man Loves a Woman	LaConnie Taylor-Jones	$6.99
When Dreams Float	Dorothy Elizabeth Love	$8.95
When I'm With You	LaConnie Taylor-Jones	$6.99
When Lightning Strikes	Michele Cameron	$6.99
Where I Want To Be	Maryam Diaab	$6.99
Whispers in the Night	Dorothy Elizabeth Love	$8.95
Whispers in the Sand	LaFlorya Gauthier	$10.95
Who's That Lady?	Andrea Jackson	$9.95
Wild Ravens	AlTonya Washington	$9.95
Yesterday Is Gone	Beverly Clark	$10.95
Yesterday's Dreams, Tomorrow's Promises	Reon Laudat	$8.95
Your Precious Love	Sinclair LeBeau	$8.95

Order Form

Mail to: Genesis Press, Inc.
P.O. Box 101
Columbus, MS 39703

Name _____
Address _____
City/State _____ Zip _____
Telephone _____

Ship to (if different from above)
Name _____
Address _____
City/State _____ Zip _____
Telephone _____

Credit Card Information
Credit Card # _____ ☐ Visa ☐ Mastercard
Expiration Date (mm/yy) _____ ☐ AmEx ☐ Discover

Qty.	Author	Title	Price	Total

Use this order form, or call 1-888-INDIGO-1	
Total for books	_____
Shipping and handling: $5 first two books, $1 each additional book	_____
Total S & H	_____
Total amount enclosed	_____

Mississippi residents add 7% sales tax

Visit www.genesis-press.com for latest releases and excerpts.